I0602020

THE MANY FENTANYL ADDICTED WRAITHS OF SAULT SAINTE MARIE

MICHAEL SAUVE

TP

TAILWINDS PRESS

Tailwinds Press
P.O. Box 2283, Radio City Station
New York, NY 10101-2283
www.tailwindspress.com

Published in the United States of America
ISBN: 978-1-7356016-4-9
1st ed. 2021

This work was produced with the support of the City of Toronto through the Toronto Arts Council.

The Many Fentanyl Addicted Wraiths of Sault Sainte Marie

For Irene Bennett

There are a thousand and one reasons, but they all boil down to a single reason: we left because our parents counselled us to leave, begged and pleaded with us to leave, even ordered us to leave. Only yonder in the big city, they insisted, could one be a truly big person; here in this town one could be no more than a large fish in a tiny pond. Better to be the tail of a lion in a great city, than the head of a jackal in Sault Sainte Marie.

— Morley Torgov, "A Good Place to Come From"

Well, a childish dream is a deathless need
And a noble truth is a sacred creed

— Bob Dylan, "Tweedle Dee and Tweedle Dum,"
Love and Theft

The following, along with all otherwise-attributed italicized content to follow, is excerpted from *The Story of Baw-a-ting, being the annals of Sault Ste. Marie* by Sir Edward Henry Capp, published in 1903 by Sault Star Press:

> The air is full of mysticism, and as the roar of the train dies away and night sets in there grows on the ear the importunate boom of the tossing Sault as a voice eager to tell the story of its flowing and of the men who have come and gone.
>
> The humble work is now hesitatingly launched with the one hope that it may be received with tolerance by all who have learned to love the Canadian town at the foot of the rapids.

Gone from the Station Mall was the Sears, once our Macy's or Saks Fifth Avenue. New to the Station Mall was an uncarpeted Lazer Tag arena. Gone were the carpets in general. Gone was half the movie theatre. The remaining half would never show anything but cartoons or action movies ever again, if the current marquee was any indication. Gone were the specialty stores that sold puzzles and tole paints. New to the mall were the discount stores that sold tinfoil, barbecue lighters, and Happy Valentine Glass Roses, the accoutrements of the town's new hobby.

Through my formative years the Station Mall had been the hub of our social lives. The Ubetcha for NVT trivia and 1,500-calorie fry baskets. The Sears beds for man-on-man ironic frottage until rousted by aggrieved and heteronormative Sears functionaries. The CDs bought with fists of nickels and quarters. *Aneurysm* and *Big Shiny Tunes*. I could luck out and run into Adelle Salituri and remark incisively about price points at the Pantorama. Her laughter and forehead would keep my Saliturian dream plodding along for a few lonely nights, pillow clutched to my chest. The mall could give me that. The tiles alone could break your heart. The radio jingle knew the score: "The Station Mall / the centre of it all."

Big Rog was handed a toonie. He offered me a knowing look.

I'd argued that a toonie was an egregious asking point. Rog insisted that quarters would never cut it because few mall customers had money to spare, fewer were charitable, and the remainder bore Big Rog personal ill-will. The ask had to account for all this and still be commensurate to our end goal of one hundred and sixty collective dollars. It seemed Rog's time working as a call centre man had not been a total wash. He'd picked up the donor relations logic necessary to keep him pushing forward in life.

With no real economy to mooch off of in Sault Sainte Marie, the mall was the only place where the dope sick could obtain items of economic worth, such as an entire rack of parkas from the Sportc Chek; or quotidian items like tampons and diapers, as junkies, turns out, have living, peeing, and pooping offspring, as do their drug dealers.

Figures from the underclass such as Big Rog had seen the decline's gradient steepening for nearly a decade. The aging population remained oblivious until the approximate time of the great axe robbery. One early Monday morning some amphetaminic axe-men had axed their way into the closed mall, axed into the Charm Jewellery store, axed into some display cases, and then hooped and hollered out to the parking lot, axes akimbo and agleam with DeBeers diamond shards. A couple were caught. The others were presumed axing their way into the homes of the most vulnerable on the nightly. There is something really distasteful about robbers using axes instead of guns. You figured they'd have to aim that axe pretty accurately at your head. You figured they probably had to practise. You figured an axe-blow was really an all-or-nothing proposition.

"This fentanyl stuff," the aged had said over their *Sault Stars* the next morning, sneering as they sneered at all the world's indecipherable innovations, as though fentanyl were a granddaughter's nudes shared to her entire Science class over Snapchat. That must have been a sad Tuesday for some city councilman when he first rushed through the mall rather than lingering over coffees and discussing the formidable Soo Greyhounds as he'd been doing his whole life, when the mall's only larceny fit neatly under the banner of "late-stage retail capitalism." That councilman's baseline contentedness had been some prerequisite to play the game in Sault Sainte Marie. Otherwise you saw the slush in the mall vestibule and heard cold snow crunching underfoot and wondered, "Why here?" Whereas the Sault lifers with their smiling eyes would have said, "The Sault is a pretty special place," and of course it was due to a lack of context, but they had still believed with all the Mystery of Faith that is fetishized at Our Lady of Good Counsel Cathedral, which is no cathedral at all, possessing all the architectural aesthetics of an abandoned elementary school.

We paced, blew our noses, and ran water over our hands in the handicapped bathroom for fifteen minutes before Rog received a text.

"He's not coming. Guess we're out of luck," said Big Rog. "He said maybe tomorrow he can get ten percs in the morning."

"Where's ten percs going to get me?" I asked.

"Ten percs total," responded Big Rog.

I'd exposed my unconscious intention to circumvent Rog at the earliest opportunity. Rog, used to this sort of thing, did not hold it against me.

"Might be able to get some in the west end though," said Rog.

The mall and its memories weren't yet through with me. Exiting through the mall's westernmost slush vestibule I encountered Adelle Salituri, grade eight mistress of friend affection and inevitable rejection, and then an ersatz actual friend throughout high school, seating partner through all five high school English classes, causing the crush to continue from Willy Loman through to Winston Smith, all while we'd feverishly messaged on the then popular ICQ. Here was a girl with whom I'd compared price points at Pantorama. A girl with whom I'd attended birthday pool parties, where she'd worn bathing suits that I can still recall, particularly one that was almost see-through. More to me than the flesh occupying a blue and borderline translucent bathing suit, she had been funny, like the time we'd been returning from the Pizza Hut in the neighbouring town, and we'd passed the local reprobate establishment, and she'd said then, of the Nicolet Tavern, "It's my favourite tavern!" in that child voice she was so good at.

I cast my eyes slushward. I didn't want her to see me in Roger's company, in my salt-stained jogging pants. She was pushing one of those double-child strollers. With little to do in Sault Sainte Marie, you put all your chips on family life, or you made a career elsewhere, or you went the Big Rog route and sloshed around in the pig pen of degeneracy until you found yourself thoroughly mired.

"Oh my god, hi," she said.

The stroller did not stop rolling, however. I couldn't blame her for not wanting to interact with Big Rog, given his prison record, his history of transgressions with young people, his perceived aura of menace and malignity. My real fear was that she did not want to interact with me.

Out in the -20°C night, Big Rog remarked, "She's still pretty hot. Some of these Italian girls never lose it, eh?"

"How do I look?" I asked him. "Be honest."

"A lot greyer than she probably remembers."

We biked to the west end. Big Rog had biked these slick hills for the entirety of his adult life and operated like some bipedal mountain goat. Not being accustomed to ice biking, this nearly killed me on both a cardiovascular and a slip-and-fall level.

Rog entered the house without knocking. It was that kind of house. Two girls sat on a couch. One looked no older than my thirteen-year-old sister Maisie. The other looked a little more mature, or was at least slathered in a greater degree of Dollarama makeup.

The house had that sadness of stale cigarette smoke and empty pop cans. A life cobbled together with hot dog water and Stouffer's single-serving pot pies. Sold for $1 each at No Frills, these pies contained 38 grams of mostly saturated fat and 1080 mg of sodium. A gram bag of salt per pie. The cost was worn bodily, not monetarily. There'd been parents here once, probably, to heat the pies. There'd been those kids who weren't reared even remotely right and were always too loud and too hyper and played too violently. Kids that couldn't even be reprimanded properly because the parents themselves were full of rage and Stouffer's sodium and Labatt's Blue or, god forbid, Maximum Ice strong beer. The salt and the beer made the parents miserable over the SSM public transit system's dwindling services. Until one day the stepfather leaves for some western tar pit that's rumoured to be hiring low men. Until the mother finds a new man.

The rent keeps getting paid somehow, always does in these places. And so some teenager takes over the house that was never a home and sets out his Sacklerian awning and lives the only way he knows how (pot pies, cigarettes, low-level desperation.)

The younger girl appeared nervous. Here were two thirty-year-old men encroaching upon her social life. Whenever could her mother's "running with the wrong crowd'" concerns have rung truer? The eyeshadowed girl took the opposite tact.

"Rog, how's it going bud?" she asked.

Rog hugged her. This struck me as inappropriate given some of the specific charges on Rog's criminal record. But then, as we intended to buy opioids from these teens, I had to concede that normal teen-30yo man relations were out the window.

A young man slightly older than the girls emerged from his bedroom, ceremonial blunt in mouth, pants seized between his knees and posterior, mitigating the whole point of pants, requiring his belt to perform a function it was never designed for. We handed him some bills and some loonies and some quarters. To his credit, this new avatar of Sault Sainte Marie entrepreneurial bravura refused the nickels, if not the dimes. He handed us six home-pressed pills.

As I remounted my childhood bicycle, Rog squared me in the eyes for a sincere exchange.

"Bro, I have to warn you, there might be some fentanyl in these pills."

"Rog, friend, I would be steamed if there was anything but fentanyl in them."

"Don't say that, man. I lost too many good friends for

joking about that."

"Withdrawn," I said, but Rog did not get this *mot juste*, so I continued, "Any chance it would be carfentanyl."

"What's that?"

"Elephant kind."

"Oh shit. Stronger you mean?"

"What in your experience, Big Rog, possesses greater body mass? A human man or an elephant-sized man? Why carfentanyl is the kind that killed Prince."

Rog whistled as a man gripped by a previous generation's obsession might have over a Chevrolet's horsepower. We parted ways.

No one was awake in my family home. I went to my creepy room. It hadn't changed since I'd departed for the University of Toronto, left by my mother to stand as some shrine to the young man I'd been and would never be again.

I swallowed the first pill. I remained, like so many of my generation, and to the disdain of your more spectral and stereotypical dope fiends, an oral user. Fifteen minutes passed with no relief. I took the second pill. Some relief but not what I'd anticipated. I took the third, overdosed, and that was it for me as a corporeal, living, and breathing human being upon this too sad earth.

I found myself suspended above my body. In the early days of an opioid habit, before disposable funds are one's every waking concern, there's time to read. Thus familiar with the pioneering works of Dr. Raymond Moody, I knew I was having the textbook near-death experience. Soon the NDE would conclude and I would return to my body, shamed but chastened, alive if never quite thrilled to be so. I only hoped the NDE concluded before ambulances were called, medical costs incurred by the province, emotional costs wrought upon my parents, and so forth.

As the NDE stretched on, I decided to make the most of the experience. These open-eye visuals were sought and blogged about by virginal psychonauts of all stripe. It would make for an interesting story during some subjunctive retirement to the coffee-slurping NA circuit. As looking down upon my physical being became something of a drag, I experimented with how far my observing wraith-like entity might venture.

I went to my brother's room, where he was sleeping and respiratory. I wondered how long a man could go without respiration. Surely not longer than an hour or two. My knowledge of the human body was limited at this time. Rolling the carfentanyl dice on a daily basis engenders a willful ignorance of the autonomic processes. I preferred to contemplate NDEs and underground bases, moth men and black-eyed kids.

My brother's room had no posters or team pennants or anything that would have adorned the teenage male abode during my adolescence spent in the abutting room. I guess by 2018 pop stars were worshipped by few other than the *eTalk* red carpet team and those immobile sufferers cruelly parked before the *eTalk* broadcasts by overworked nursing home staff. Who did these boys worship instead? YouTubers who subtly urged ethno-states? Adult men who discoursed on "ethics in gaming journalism" for a living? Could a parent even acquire of such a man, as a Christmas gift? Could a parent go to the Station Mall and ask, "My son likes Pooty Pie. Any posters of him?"

I checked on my mother, Claudette. Obviously respiratory as she was loudly snoring. This was the reason my father slept in a separate bedroom. Checked on him and yes sir, respiratory.

My NDE was getting old. I didn't want to force the issue. If I floated above the non-respiratory body long enough, surely I'd be absorbed back into it. The heart-stopping characteristics of the (car)fentanyl would have raun their course and I'd nod off to a lovely slumber. I'd meet Big Rog for the next day's slog and everything would be fine. I'd fall into a routine: visiting the mall, visiting the low-slung trousers kid, eventually usurping him of his operation, setting up a minor empire in which I used Big Rog as muscle due to the menacing personality traits unfairly associated with him after his time spent in the penitentiary.

I aimed my consciousness into my corporeal husk. Nothing doing. I thought I might enter through the eyes. As is commonly remarked, these constitute the window to the soul. I did not like the look of the bluish hue creeping into my corporeal visage, nor the slackening of the neck and cheek flesh, nor yet my tongue's imbecilic protuberance.

I wondered if perhaps some air would benefit my floating wraith perspective. I floated through the door and into the -3°C night. A warm front had moved in. Snow-mist rained down through me. I merged with this mist, used this mist as a conveyance of sorts. I accelerated upwards to interface with clouds, and then stars, achieving a sense of star matter. Overwhelmed by all that, I headed back to the back yard I'd played with the neighbour Gerrard girls in, with its fire pit and rope swing, its many ruts and grassless patches, its bag of frozen soil left out stupidly since the summer. I heard the neighbour's baby crying. The neighbours were no Gerrards, who had abandoned me so long ago. Maybe that had planted the seed. Maybe it was the warmth of those Gerrardian girls that an opioid offered some meagre facsimile of, like a superimposition of Ingrid Bergman's face over a frame of otherwise dingy celluloid. I could see the flapping wing of a seagull that had failed to migrate if seagulls even do such a thing, failed to leave Sault Sainte Marie sensibly as the Gerrards had. I flew to the ostentatiously named International Bridge. I knew then the whole gloom of the town, felt those Sault Sainte Marie fentanyl OD blues. Not that you needed a fentanyl OD to have the Sault Sainte Marie blues. It was how the average family man felt picking up a bucket of greasy spuds at Frank's Fried Chicken.

I visited the home of Big Rog, drifted into his bedroom that had changed little since his own high school years. There lay Big Rog, also bluer than usual, also non-respiratory. "Big Rog," I sub-vocalized. No response. I hoped some living relation of Big Rog would call an ambulance or a mortician to dispose of Big Rog's quickly-bloating GG Allin corpse.

What now? What now?

I floated into Big Rog's kitchen, his mother's kitchen really, the only nice room in the house with its orange-brown tiles and chairs that called to mind *Family Ties* or the brown warmth of the great 80s sitcoms Big Rog must have also viewed in syndication.

How did all this Sault Sainte Marie violence, all this Sault Sainte Marie dissatisfaction, emerge from these brown-tiled kitchens? All those ancient footsteps of Big Rog and his also (2014) OD'd sister falling on these tiles in the Easter morning before breakfast.

It dawned on me that I was still high. Though my body had absorbed the poisonous fentanyl or carfentanyl dose, my NDE-experiencing wraith consciousness was reaping the benefits. I'd long sought to differentiate what of the opiate pleasure was the physical comfort of wrapping oneself up in a blanket of nociceptional safety, and what was the absence of the psyche's unending pain: the grade eleven rejections that never really leave us but just run on in the background like malignant anti-happiness software. Bodiless, I knew the answer. Physical comfort can only ever be a manifestation of psychical comfort.

I checked on my own deathly tableaux and encountered a cheerless scene, the underside of the death-relief coin, the collateral pain that keeps suicidal altruistics living and begrudgingly breathing—it was the face of my brother, inches above the skin and slackening muscle of my own. He was scream-whispering, "C'mon bro, c'mon bro wake up."

The camaraderie implicit in the word "bro" was hard to take. David had been cold and avoidant in the few weeks since I'd returned home from Toronto. He'd heard horror stories from my father: I was there to bleed everyone dry, waste all the tinfoil, and burn his borrowed jeans with dropped cigarettes.

Now David was in a bind. He didn't want to raise trouble over what might be a mere nod-out when maybe he thought non-respiratory nod-outs were the norm. He couldn't let me die on his watch either. David turned on all the lights. He held back an eyelid and shone his phone flashlight into an unresponding iris. "Mom!" he yelled through the ceiling. My mother pounded down the creaky steps. "Call an ambulance," she told David before employing her quasi-medical training as a vet tech to check for a pulse and administer some ineffective CPR.

My father arrived and said, "Oh Christ," equal parts "well-it's-finally-come-to-this-and-here-in-our-own-home-amidst-our-as-yet-unruined-children-no-less" and genuine sadness. He lit a cigarette though in-house smoking was forbidden. This man who'd raised me, surprised me with both an Easton hockey stick and a PlayStation one Christmas, with whom I'd rarely shared a meaningful adult exchange, let alone any kind of approach to living in the world—he nonsensically applied an icepack to my forehead. My sister kept knocking at the door, sounding more annoyed than concerned. When the sirens spoke in the distance she got the hint. The ambulance made good time, I felt, even if time was starting to feel rather subjective.

A paramedical administration of Narcan did nothing. My observing wraith knew the Narcan's window of efficacy was long past. If my observing wraith had wanted Narcan administered I could have dimmed the lights in ghostly fashion or creaked the floorboards in such a way as to demand investigation. I'd done none of these things, not wanting to spoil the high, or perhaps having been lulled into a false sense of security by Dr. Raymond Moody's pioneering accounts of the NDE experience.

I was anticipating a trip to the hospital, really was. As I would later learn in my many hours spent haunting the Korah Public Library, the *Deceased Patient Standard* had been replaced in 2009 by the *Vital Signs Absent (Transportation) Standard* by the Ministry of Health and Long Term Care. The relevant change: no sense tying up hospital beds and ambulances with a bunch of literal stiffs.

A third-rate team of certified death-acknowledgers

dropped by to make it official. I was sent to a holding area at the funeral home. I wraith-whistled that old Daniel Johnston number *Funeral Home*, one of the many torch songs about Daniel Johnston's beloved Laurie, the girl that had barely acknowledged him let alone loved him back, but had occasionally been nice to him. The song gave me a sense of purpose. Rather than follow what remained of my flesh and my bones to some grey box, rather than absorb all the guilt associated with familial grief permutations, I would visit Adelle.

I knew the neighbourhood and the house from Facebook pictures. I ducked my wisps beneath her transom, floated up some stairs, ignored a gurgling baby or two, and found her waking up next to her husband. His presence robbed me of whatever romantic purpose had brought me to her bungalow. It was this way for all the lovelorn, all the also-rans of yesteryear. Write your great song *Girl of My Dreams* or *Funeral Home* for your Laurie and at best she's flattered; at worst a Form 14 notice of motion for a restraining order is brought before a justice of the peace. Regardless she goes on to marry the Accountant and provider and Good Man, or in Daniel Johnston's case, an actual funeral home director, and we the also-rans are left to pine until pining becomes a comic proposition, until all that remains is some shimmer of the night she sat on your lap in some over-crowded van going to a football game or something.

Adelle Salituri's alarm sounded. Her skin was as brown as ever. All these Italians in town had no need for sunshine. People used to say she resembled Britney Spears. A nascent film buff in those days, I'd thought she looked like Barbara Stanwyck. Prized more for my wit than my mediocre backup basketball skills, I hoped to one day be her Preston Sturges, to write all those great lines that she could say in our own *The Lady Eve*.

Adelle rose from her bed. I allowed my wraith ions to briefly occupy the warm recess she'd left behind, but then I was essentially lying beside the Certified Public Accountant, which was unfair to the both of us.

In the adjoining bathroom my wraith-particles mixed with the shower steam. Though I had the tact to provide her with some privacy by remaining outside the curtain, Adelle Salituri must have been breathing me in to some extent. Here, I rationalized, was a type of congress, more Eucharistic than any crass Soo insertion, where the most popular euphemism for sex has always been *wheeling*. The ionic congress was something I could think of as a second communion.

And did this spectral communion create a particular sadness in her eyes as she later prepared pea and sweet potato mush for her many babies? Or was that sadness always in her eyes because she had stayed in Sault Sainte Marie instead of leveraging her beauty to become a cast member in some cruise ship production of *Grease*? As the CPA poured cereal and spoke about who-could-ever-care-what, I thought it best to leave.

Seeking a palate cleanser of natural beauty, I boarded the first morning trip of the Agawa Canyon Tour Train. I saw the few tourists who'd been duped into travelling to the Soo for the photographic opportunities this train yielded. How could photography ever hope to opiate these tourist psyches properly? "Your photographs will get you nowhere," I sub-vocalized at one man, "And if you'd bothered to apply the 'population density filter' to any choropleth map you'd find this train is taking you to the exact middle of nowhere. Why not deboard while you can, visit the west end instead, and try some carfentanyl on for size, deadly sure, but what true relief ever would not be?"

From every building blew exhaust, the heat from inside mixing with the cold of outside. The warm front was gone and it was -30°C without the wind chill. In Toronto I resented how a real -7 became a -14 by including the wind-chill without mention. Torontonians rarely got -14 anymore, so they'd make these inflationary attempts that fooled no one. Whereas in Sault Sainte Marie you wake up and it's -30 and you put on a hooded sweatshirt and walk to your car, and then, god willing, you drive to your job at the Roberta Bondar Centre, our hub of Ontario Government make-work employments.

The private sector struggles here. A giant anchor store in a mall will turn into a *Halloween Store!* The stated intention for the *Halloween Store!* is to keep up with the seasonal times by transitioning into a *Christmas Store!* and then an *Easter Store!* When it fails within the first month, the giant *Halloween Store!* banner remains up into June and July and through the next *Halloween!* as a cruel joke on everyone.

A well-meaning businessman will get the bright idea to offer "something for the young people." He'll renovate an

80,000-square-foot former Zellers and make it a sports bar, an arcade, a nightclub, and the city's best butter chicken restaurant. It's trying to be all things to all people, to give each of the young something, and so it can give them nothing. It sits nearly empty on this Friday evening, with the exception of six men of absurd musculature making quarter-hourly trips to the washroom, en masse, before playing the free throw arcade game with borrowed dopamine to spare. The one waitress is absurdly pretty, with all that French and Italian blood, maybe some Métis. Who can be certain where the darkness of the Sault Sainte Marie angel face originates? She's got to be the best that has not yet migrated south. A 44-year-old man in his elevator repairman coveralls, desiring proximity to this girl and also a lot of carbohydrates, is eating two poutines. He couldn't even order them consecutively, just wanted them both right at that moment, as though one poutine could never be enough. The waitress is too pretty for this two-poutine baloney.

She could be making $500 a night at any The Keg in any suburban big box hellhole. Get your town a The Keg and at least you are above the indignities inflicted by any one man's poor business instincts. And if the poutine man was anything like me, by the time he finished the poutines he'd be afflicted with those old Sault Sainte Marie blues; he'd think of his union brothers repairing elevators in other, bigger towns, and as the cheese curds and the gravy turned to chyme and then bolus, he'd be *awaking to the unhappy fact that he is not progressing but rather losing in the fight for place.* He's increasingly *jealous of the more successful rival or rivals and the spirit quickly develops into hate.*

Another man, roughly the same age, but quite obviously

worse off, was wearing a baby blue FUBU jersey manufactured in 1998. Upscale fashion boutiques are sometimes opened on Queen Street to offset the lack of reputable clothiers. These struggle since the only men with expendable income are the old men who wear hunting jackets with no sense of irony; have probably in fact gone hunting within the week. Older women, often indistinguishable from the old men except for the fashion choices they might make, still manage to neglect these choices, wearing a leftover Berkley snowboard jacket from the days when a child enlivened their home. They pull up the jacket's wonky zipper and speak of the greener economic pastures their boy has left for. And the woman's semi-grieving friend will issue that ancient Sault Sainte Marie lament, "There's nothing here for the young people."

Some of the old ladies in this town have known each other for seventy years. They all have that wry smile and those eyes wrinkly from a lifetime of smiling over nothing. Maybe their Sault Sainte Marie was better. Maybe 1950s and 1960s conformity made it feel like Manhattan. Maybe men wore ties when they weren't hunting. In my time we merely affected the attitudes and fashions dictated by NBC's Thursday Night Must See lineup. Through it all we were cruelly aware that while our prettiest girls were a passable approximation of peak Jennifer Aniston, our sharpest wits would never be Frasier Crane. We would be hard-pressed to come up with some quipping Chandler. And yet these ladies smiled on.

I wondered then if I might somehow pair my soul to one of these smiling ladies. If it could be done with wireless speakers, why not a damaged soul? Maybe haunt the halls of the nursing home, find some old bag happy even in dementia and diapers, wirelessly pair my soul to hers, and then when the reaper creeps his head in the door, tilts his scythe downwards so it will fit through . . . well perchance the reaper is busy that day, dozen souls to reap all the way to Temiskaming Shores and back, so he mistakes my soul for the contented bag's, reaps it, sends it to the bardo, and then I'm born back into Sault Sainte Marie in 1948 only to grow up hard enough that a TV should be a luxury, nothing but an orange in my stocking come Christmas, and then they land men on the moon and by the end of this life people are talking into Google Homes as though she myself, the reincarnated old bag, feels like she is living on that very Apollo mission of 1969. I would see Bob Dylan when he came to the Memorial Gardens in 1991 and be disappointed. I'd grow roses. I'd be given a china doll as a five-year-old and appreciate it as no (in the gross parlance of clickbait sites) *'90s kid* ever appreciated a Super Nintendo. I'd put ribbons on the head of a fair-haired grandchild. I'd be fairly oblivious by the time Mortimer Sackler of Purdue Pharma got the bright idea to finally offer something for the young people (synthetic opioidal joys.) Ten years would pass, then forty, and I'd meet with the other wrinkle-eyed old bags and say, "Where does the time go?" But I'd know. I'd know that the time goes into our hearts.

After all this pontification I returned to my parents' house to take in the grieving process. There I was saddened to observe a bare minimum of grieving going on.

My father sat on the back porch completing a crossword puzzle. After his own father had succumbed to Alzheimer's, he'd learned this pastime might keep the scourge of demented aging at bay. All winter he sat in the sun-drenched living room. In the summer he spent his days on the porch. My mother often remarked that he "wasn't making the most of his retirement" or "didn't know what to do with himself."

My brother David was playing *Call of Duty: Black Ops 4* with a look of dire concentration on his face. I gave him the benefit of the doubt, assuming he might need to occupy his mind. But then his team captured some strategically-valuable elevator shaft and he yelled into his headset with what I considered an altogether inappropriate degree of enthusiasm.

My sister was engaged in the proceeding FB group chat:

Maisie Kay: Guys did you hear about Mellissa Gladstone?

Jay Allysa: I did. And your brother! Oh my god are you ok?

Maisie Kay: Ya I knew about my brother since this morning so I'm getting over that cuz I never really saw him since I was young and he'd only been home a couple days but I just heard about Mellissa now, lol.

Sam Caputo: Did Mellissa die like your brother, a slip and fall?

Maisie Kay: Yeah pretty sure that was just a cover story my mom gave me. Saw Mellissa's mom post about fentanill and I know my brother did that too and you don't slip and fall in your bedroom do u.

Sam Caputo: WHAT??? Is he going to be ok?

Andie Tomlinson: OMG we already all knew he died you idiot!!!

[ANDIE TOMLINSON REMOVED SAM CAPUTO FROM THE GROUP CHAT]

Jay Alyssa: She's so dumb.

Andie Tomlinson: Finally the excuse we needed to get her out of the chat tho. So sorry Maze!

Maisie Kay: It's okay she's just stupid she didn't mean anything.

Andie Tomlinson: I meant for your brother but the same thing.

Due to the dearth of detail in the chat, I was guessing that neither Maisie nor her friends had read the newspaper or seen a link posted online. The fact that 0/4 local youths had even glimpsed its front page didn't bode well for the future readership of the *Sault Star*. I had delivered that paper from the ages of twelve to eighteen. My father had bought colour ads in its weekly automotive section. If you scored a goal in house league it made the dense little column of house league happenings. It had been, since the nineteeth century, an institution.

Thirty papers could strain my back. Now it was a page and a half of local content, what few ads they could sell, and a few wire stories that had appeared twenty-three hours previous on this thing called the Internet. When once there'd been columnists, honest-to-god gainfully-employed columnists who wrote nothing but columns in a town of 80,000; and two sports reporters; a business reporter; and a city hall reporter. Only three were left standing, including Bob Stickman, author of this article concerned with my demise:

Tainted Drugs Feared After Three Monday Night Overdoses

Three people died of suspected fentanyl overdoses on Monday night.

The three deceased are Tom Astaire, 30, Roger Palombi, 29, and Mellissa Gladstone, 13.

The slain three may have received the deadly and controversial opioid from the same source.

Safety advocates are urging opiate users to take extra precautions.

"It's extremely frightening," said Deb Martin, spokesperson for the Concerned Sault Sainte Marie Residents Against the Opioid Epidemic Who Are Nonetheless Advocating For Safe Injection Sites Cooperative.

"And the worst part," said the controversial CSSM-RAOEWNAFSIS spokesperson, "is that many of these addicts are asking for fentanyl by name. If any good is to come out of last night, maybe it will change that. I'm afraid it won't due to the high demand for pharmaceutical opiates in town and the low quality of the town's regular heroin."

Martin then reiterated her controversial position that the Soo's overdoses would lower rather than skyrocket with taxpayer-funded management of taxpayer-funded injection sites. Many voices on the crisis, including Chief Douglas Bindi of the SSM Police's Fentanyl Crackdown Unit, strongly oppose the safe injection sites.

Bindi, formerly of the SSM Minor Sex Abuse Unit, said at a press conference, "If these dope-dealing scum think that that 13-year-old girl's blood is the only blood that will run on these streets, then these scums don't know much about Bad Doug Bindi and the current policing climate in Sault Sainte Marie."

Bindi's comments were then walked back by the SSM-PD-FCU's press liaison Diane DiGiulio, who stressed, "If you or someone you know is suffering from fentanyl overdosing issues please call emergency services immediately."

As of February 23, these are the twelfth, thirteenth, and fourteenth opioid-related deaths of 2018. The previous annual high was 18.

I went to my mother's room and was relieved to find her looking at an infant picture of me: swaddled in a head scarf, picking rhubarb—there I was, her little son. I hoped to comfort this woman in whatever electromagnetic wraith fashion I might be capable of, but was distracted then by an unmistakable instinct warning me of another wraith upon the premises.

I soon found the trespasser in Maisie's room. To my eye,

this wraith was creepily observing Maisie, who was dressed in a pair of volleyball shorts and a cut-off T-shirt that would only be revealing to a wraith with all the wrong intentions who was capable of working the angles.

"I'm afraid I'll have to ask you to leave," I said.

"Came to see if you were here and I got lost," said Big Rog.

And by *said*, let me clarify that there was no mouth movement or exhalation of breath. These words were communicated telepathically.

"Likely story," I said, "Why don't we convene this wraith conference in my dad's workshop."

"Wreath conference?"

"Ghost conference," I said.

Big Rog gave me the rundown of how he'd spent the last two days.

Upon the occasion of his OD, Rog was visited by the Wraith of his older sister Meredith. Rather than towards the light, Meredith had taken Rog to his favourite places to comfort him: the bowling alley, the drive-in movie theatre that had long since closed, the mall food court. Rog offered a wan smile that intimated, "How could these be the places? How could a food court be the setting for the finest moments in a life?"

The Wraith of Rog, also still high, had asked Meredith, "Is this heaven?"

Wearing her always-bitch-face expression, Meredith sub-vocalized, "Do I look high to you?"

As Big Rog recounts, she did not. She had the resigned look of defeat she'd worn throughout her living years, with the brief exception of her preteen years during which it's hard not to be at least curious about the world, and in her final years when opioids had superseded Meredith's need for either curiosity or happiness.

"You're going to come down," the Wraith of Meredith

had warned, "Slower, very gradual. I guess cause no liver and stuff, but just as bad, worse actually."

"How long?" asked Big Rog.

"Started sneezing a couple weeks in. Took me about a year to get right. Now there's just the boredom."

"How'd you get through it? Ghost Suboxone?" asked Big Rog. "Tell me there's ghost subs."

She'd gotten through by attending spectral NA meetings with her fellow narcotics-withdrawing wraiths. Rog described a scene at Our Lady of Good Counsel that I had a difficult time believing, and so, given the light-speed we were capable of travelling at, I suggested Big Rog should show rather than tell.

We arrived to find a few dozen wraiths floating above the church aisles. Although incapable of drinking let alone holding a coffee, coffee is such an integral part of the NA experience that those assembled had manifested their wraith wisps to resemble hands holding a cup, with smaller wisps manifesting as steam rising from their cups.

I recognized one such wraith, Rex, as a former mechanic at my dad's garage. During my final years of high school this man had been the bane of my father's existence. A carjack had given out and crushed Rex's femur, patella, and tibia. Thing was, this was the fifth improbable accident to befall Rex that month alone. Previous accidents had all been prevented or at least mitigated by third-party intervention. In the case of his leg crushing, witness testimony stated that Rex had intentionally kicked the jack out from under the Ford Fiesta in question. While the witnesses weren't able to speculate on why a man might do such a thing, my father's lawyer was free to speculate exactly why: for the insurance claim. This was 2003. Having less knowledge of the ways and means of the opioidial, the judge couldn't yet fathom how a man might willingly invite a quarter ton of Detroit steel upon his lower quadrant. The judge couldn't yet understand that such a crushing meant not only a life-sustaining insurance payout, but also a life-enrichening OxyContin supply.

The Wraith of Rex was orating passionately, "Thing I always hated most was that show *Intervention*. The intervener comes in all high and mighty and says, 'Look at your cousin's face. Your cousin loves you and lets you live rent free in his garage.' Cousin was probably fine with the whole setup. Think that cousin never did a couple lines up in the garage? And there's the cousin having to go by the interventioners' playbook and look all sad and remorsing."

A few wraithly nods from the audience to commiserate that the cousin, like all the cousins of the world, had definitely snorted a few lines up in the garage and surely even bought a few dozen bags himself, but no he wouldn't be owning up to that with the cameras rolling because it wasn't he the cousin who'd fucked up so bad that a dying cable network was spending tens of thousands of dollars a week to film him.

"I always preferred the first part when it showed the interventionee guy, the addict that is, on a wild binge up in the garage, like maybe he'd run out of blow so he was inhaling from a can of spray paint 'cause that's his backup. I always rooted for them to keep that binge going as long as possible. That should have told me I was headed for trouble," said the Wraith of Rex.

"I heard that one of those intervener guys fell off the wagon and went on a wild binge of his own, just booze and gambling, but don't think that combo doesn't get pretty ugly, you know like placing thousand-dollar lightning bets on a meaningless Phoenix Suns game on a Wednesday night. I always hoped they'd do an episode on him, show him sucking off fat old truckers for scratch ticket money, and then show him scratching the scratch tickets and losing and then looking into the camera all remorsing himself and saying, 'Guess it's back out to the parking lot,' and then it shows him putting on his lip gloss and entering another truck and that's the tag they need to take it to commercial."

Some chuckling and polite applause from the assembled community of narcotics-addicted wraiths.

"You know, I like to tell these stories of when I was alive because it reminds me how much better off I am now, free from all that anger, free from drugs, and one hundred and fifty days sober . . . " said the Wraith of Rex.

"Hundred fifty days dead," joked one of NAW wits.

The crowd all sub-vocalized hearty laughter at this, much heartier than the laughter that greeted Rex's interventionist schadenfreude.

"Dead and sober," said the Wraith of Rex, "Funny cause the *Intervention* jerks always threatened, 'You want to end up dead?' Answer to that should have always been yes."

At meeting's end the wraiths congregated around a coffee pot that wasn't really a coffee pot but just more wraith wisps that one of the addicts was manifesting from her own personal wisps in order to foster a sense of community.

"Big Rog, nice to see you bud," said the Wraith of Rex, "Who's the new guy?"

Throughout litigation the living Rex had threatened to kill not just my father, but also my fifteen-year-old self, and also my infant brother, and even my newborn baby sister, so I chose to fly off. Big Rog followed.

"That place gives me the creeps," I said.

"Same here," said Big Rog, "Probably because we're still high and they aren't."

"Isn't that always the way?" I asked.

"Want to go hang out at the bowling alley then?" asked Big Rog.

"Not really. I say we go to the movies. No agency required for that. Just passive viewing. Won't be any different than in life. Except less popcorn, which might be for the best. I may pass the next several months there in fact."

Except I'd forgotten about the bisecting of our Galaxy Cinema, once our window to the world, and now nothing but tentpole movies and cartoons. Playing currently were *Tentpole 4: Canopy Rising* and *Social Agenda Cartoon*. It was like a blow to the abdomen. I have always loved the kinographic medium. One of the last essays I wrote for *Onyx* was titled *Towards a Poetics of the Kinoplex*.

"Nuts to this," I said. "I'm going to the Fox Theatre in Toronto, to Film Forum in New York, to an actual kinodrome."

"Thing about that . . . " said Big Rog.

And then Big Rog explained the boundary lines, but I did not believe in these boundary lines, so Big Rog flew me a few hundred kilometres outside of town, by Blind River, and there we ran up against some shrubs, sometimes known as a windbreak, and as we hit the windbreak we could proceed no further. Same otherworldly windbreaks formed a perimeter, for we ghosts at least, explained Big Rog. The situation was apparent. Stuck inside Sault Sainte Marie with the fentanyl OD'd wraith blues again.

Fortunately our funerals that morning took our minds off things. Mine was at the same cathedral/abandoned elementary school where the NAW meeting took place. Big Rog was thrown in a pauper's grave. Joking! His funes was at the Zion Lutheran Church.

In my parents' home my sister was trying on dresses. This struck me as inappropriate. It was not a fashion show, nor was my funeral a semi-formal.

My brother, dressed in his suit and VR helmet, was getting in a final mission of *Doom VFR (Very Fucking Real)*. Something about his PSVR headset made Maisie's dress comparisons seem downright compassionate by comparison. As he made one jerky head movement after another, as he fired his Big Fucking Gun upon demons and hellspawn, I wondered if he gave any consideration that I might be confined to the pit myself at that moment, manifesting as one of the game's Vagaries or Cacodemons or Mancubuses.

My father was in the car making sure all head and butt warmers were scorching hot. These butt warmers seemed to be my father's last remaining point of pride. Big Rog has suggested these seat warmers are the closest a 58-year-old northern Ontario man will ever come to receiving a rimjob.

My mother was redoing her mascara after it had been ruined by a weeping fit.

The expectedly-epicene priest had obviously not met or interfaced with me in preparation for my funeral, so he winged it based on a series of talking points my mother must have provided: as a youth I was passionate about reading. I had studied English at the University of Toronto. My successful publication in *Onyx: A Journal Of Mythopoesis* was mentioned as though *Onyx* were *The Paris Review*. My pioneering efforts as founder, editor, publisher, and advertising director of *Onyx* were tactfully left out.

I wasn't thrilled with the turnout. What could I expect? I'd been away from town for over a decade. I also figured the Safe Injection Site/anti-opioid turnout was divided by the funerals of Big Rog and Mellissa Gladstone. The Gladstone funeral was where the socio-emotional bread would get buttered. There the anti-opioidal needn't speak a word. They could make eye contact with the second cousin of the deceased youth, holding the gaze as if to say, "If she'd injected these orally-taken opioids safely, might dear Mellissa be alive today?"

What stung most was the absence of Adelle Salituri. Sure we'd been estranged, but wasn't that what funerals were for? To look back on those Aznavourian times we'd known? To acknowledge that we had breathed the same air for a period, crawl-spaced before we could walk, as it were, as youths, in youth with each other?

After the funes some funeral home fellows wheeled my casket into their bod-mobile (hearse). The bod-mobile conveyed my remains to the boneyard. What was this costing my parents? If I'd known this kind of cash was earmarked for my passing I'd have requested some in advance. "Leave the ghastly preparations to me!" I'd have said, and signed up for the old pine box and pauper's grave combo. Once the pauper's grave contract was signed and irrevocable, I'd say, "Look, I know it will be awkward, but just toss me in that pauper's grave. It's what I want, quite genuinely."

I would advise those thinking of dying soon to inform loved ones that you DO NOT want the premium casket. Know that the funes home folks have a mandate and it's to upsell those premiums by making your loved ones feel like cheapskates if they even mention the $1200 economy model.

The grief-stricken were encouraged to address my premium box at the boneyard. My sister threw a folded-up piece of paper in. When I later read this note, I found it poorly composed and over-reliant on *Chicken Soup for the Grieving Teen Soul* quotations. My brother stood before the casket for a moment and then knelt down to give it a couple awkward taps in the fashion of a bro hug. My father stood before the casket and briefly emitted a high-pitched mewling before kicking some dirt atop my premium model in a manly fashion. My mother chose not to address my casket in any way, which struck me as a waste of her $8400.

As my crowd dispersed, as the crank turned to lower my remains amidst the worms for eternity, the funeral procession of Big Rog happened to arrive. His procession was minimal. It consisted of his mother, some of her dirtbag relatives, and the lawyer who had represented Big Rog during his sexual interference trials/mistrials/further trials/sentencing hearings/subsequent appeals. One relative was wearing a 1995 Toronto Raptors windbreaker. I wasn't sure if this made me sadder for Big Rog, the relative, or the town as a whole.

"How's the funes going, Big Rog?" I asked.

"Kind of a bust. Priest kept calling me Reggie. My sister's was way better. Half the town showed up."

"Those were different times."

Scheduling must not have been a managerial strongpoint at this particular boneyard, for the funes procession of Mellissa Gladstone then also arrived. Now here was the gathering Rog and I had hoped for. Loved ones were literally throwing themselves to the ground in all manner of histrionics. Many outright screams of "Why? Why? Why?" In response, safe injection wonks were handing out pamphlets, the statistics on the glossy pages saying, "Here's why! Here's why! Here's why!"

Floating above it all was the Wraith of Mellissa Gladstone. Far more ethereal a wraith than Big Rog or myself, she appeared to exist like a heavenly cloud. Less wear and tear on the soul, I figured. Surely she couldn't be long for this prison trap of a Sault Sainte Marie afterlife.

"Hey Mellissa," I said, hoping to console her before Big Rog might remark inappropriately regarding the youthful élan of her wraith wisps.

"Hey guys. Sucks we all died," said the Wraith of Mellissa.

"Yeah, what have you been up to since?" I asked.

"Watching people play that claw game at the movie theatre. I've been trying to help them win."

"Any luck?" I asked.

"No, I think it's rigged."

"How was your funes?" I asked.

"Not bad. A lot of people looked like they really cared about me. It's weird because before I died no one seemed to care at all."

Big Rog went in for the consolatory hug. I was able to intercept him, but due to the immateriality of our appendages we all became bound together in one collective mass of death mist.

"Group hug!" cried the Wraith of Rog.

"Yay!" cried the Wraith of Mellissa.

At Salituri's Reception Hall I was pleased to observe a significantly better turnout for my post-funes reception. My funeral had been held on a weekday, rarely done unless you dropped dead at the precise beginning of the weekend: too soon to get your funes in by Sunday, too ghoulish to keep you un-entombed for nine long days of decomposition. Another factor dampening attendance might have been public uncertainty surrounding fentanyl-OD remains, as though all the embalming fluid and funeral cosmetology in the world couldn't undo the fentanylic or Kapoorian wear and tear on a corpse.

My father's colleagues and cronies stood by the bar making the chit-chat necessary at these functions. After an obligatory, "Sad eh?" the men would ask other pertinent questions like, "You still got that old tow truck?" For proprieties' sake, they drank slightly less than their usual allotment of six to eighteen beers.

I saw my third grade teacher Mrs. Robinson, who always inquired about me when she saw my mother at Pino's grocery store. I'm sure my mother had padded the mythopoetic narrative and omitted the more alarming truths, thus making the news that much harder to stomach for Mrs. Taylor, who'd last known me as a bright-eyed eight-year-old, and only ever heard tell of me as an upstart *Onyx* publisher.

The veterinarian who employed my mom made an appearance. Possessed of a Sophia Lorenian quality, this vet had the genetic luck to remain beautiful into her sixties. What a boon to the man who'd married her in their early twenties. Sure, they'd both been beautiful then, but as they'd observed the decline of once-equally-beautiful friends, this vet had somehow improved with age, which is suggested by popular culture to be nearly the norm, but in reality happens in less than .0015 of aging tragedies.

"You need something to take your mind off things," said the vet, Margaret Butland. "You should come with me to the casino when you're ready. We'll go to the one across the river."

Going to the casino in Sault Sainte Marie, Michigan was considered the high-end gambling option versus attending our own Gateway Casino, with its slots addicts peeing their pants, its degenerates taking advantage of the $2 appetizers and the $5 slot match coupons that they never used on slots but just immediately cashed in for a $5 windfall.

A few of my brother's friends stood looking at their phones, not entirely sure how to behave as near-adults at a post-funes gathering. My sister had asked no friends to come, and stood by the hem of my mother's dress throughout. My father appeared to be struggling against tears, flitting from one conversation to another. Checking on things at the bar. Trying to manage the situation.

Prior to the birth of my siblings, my father and I had made yearly March break trips to Haileybury, Ontario to visit his ailing parents. Almost makes me glad I'm dead, because I would never have been quite so decent to any aging loved ones, I fear, who weren't dying in my immediate vicinity. We'd make the eight-hour trek and he'd give me a budget to buy comic books. We'd drink two pops and eat four chocolate bars every time we stopped for gas because the chocolate bars were 2/$1.00 then. We'd stay at Brault's hotel, in nearby New Liskeard, even though it was more expensive and not particularly nice, because it had a pool. The days revolved around the pool. We'd go and visit my grandparents and watch their set schedule of syndicated television until that became so depressing we'd use the excuse of the pool to drive back to the hotel for a few hours. One time he took me for fries to prolong one of these pool outings and said, "Let me show you an old fry eater's trick" and then poured ketchup on the plate and salted the ketchup itself, regulating the amount of salt in each bite rather than just having the salt spill stupidly past the fries onto the ceramic plate.

I saw him give the shirt off his literal back one time and hold it against the hemorrhaging head of a bleeding man who'd crashed his motorcycle on Second Line.

I pushed him pretty hard as the imperious adolescent I was, but he seldom pushed back.

Together we'd often watched thunderstorms. We would stare at crackling fires and "shoot the breeze," as he referred to the contemplation of the mysteries.

At a snowed-in hunting camp once, despite being the smallest man with the shortest legs, he'd nearly frozen to death walking through 12 feet of snow in search of Ontario Search and Rescue. He told me his near-hypothermic death felt peaceful, like falling asleep, so maybe this gave him a sense of how death came for me.

I saw my father then, in his grief, as I'd seen him when I was a boy. My grandfather had been a milkman who delivered milk on a horse-drawn carriage. At the time of this writing there are humanistic robots and holograms interviewing each other at tech conferences, all of which is to say, things had changed a lot in the course of my father's life. I shouldn't have been so hard on him for not understanding that a mouse could be plugged into a laptop. I shouldn't have rolled my eyes every time I heard him repeat the opinion of a baseball broadcaster. I should have thought higher of the man dedicated enough to watch all that *Wheel of Fortune*. There was no apologizing for the eye rolls now, to this man who'd loved me more than he'd ever loved another human being. All I could try to do was project a benevolence as he sought to maintain the Astaire firmament in Sault Sainte Marie.

Sergeant Bad Doug Bindi arrived, kicking snow off his boots in the vestibule. It would be a busy night for him. In addition to his usual spate of low-level heads to be cracked, he had three post-funes gatherings to console and politic at.

"Devastated to hear about the spilling of your son's blood," he told my father. "With God's help I will bring pestilential woe upon the people who took your son from us, the same people who took my daughter from us . . . with God's help . . . "

Sensing Bad Doug's escalation into the realm of full-throated screaming, the tow truck-owning crony intervened and directed him to the bar. Since the overdose of Doug's daughter, Bad Doug B's affect was a complex ecosystem of righteous anger regulated only by alcohol and cocaine, and at this moment the cocaine was running the show. What

Bad Doug B needed were a couple Rye and Gingers. As the second double soothed his GABA receptors, Bad Doug settled down to the extent that he could lobby the cronies for donations to the Sault Sainte Marie Fentanyl Crackdown Unit.

"Heard the mayor set aside a pretty nice bundle for you," said one of the less cautious cronies.

Bad Doug grabbed the man by the collar and gave him the lay of the land. "That budget hardly covers the new tactical gear. Do you know what kind of arms these dealers have?"

"Limited arms, since most of them are poor or teenagers?" asked the same imprudent crony.

"You might think that," said Bad Doug B, relaxing slightly, "But that's because of your stupidity as an asshole, Rick."

The cronies all had a nervous laugh at Rick's expense.

"Some of these urban PDs have tanks. Military hand-me-downs, but still very functional. You don't think that would strike fear into some of these cartel guys?"

In my discussions with Big Rog, I'd gotten a sense of the SSM underworld, and I was pretty certain the cartel had not yet ventured this far north. The biggest players in the game were nothing more than low-level mules who had a connection in Toronto and could bring a few hundred pills into town.

"Just think, you're cooking up some fentanyl, and suddenly there's a tank crushing your step-dad's garage. Would that not send a message to the other fentanyl chefs?" asked Bad Doug.

"Thought they ordered the fentanyl from China?" said Rick.

Bad Doug Bindi's eyes indicated that his time for talking was through, and if there was time for further interaction, this time would be budgeted towards the administration of Rick's murder.

Uncharacteristic of my father's accountant Rick, he then decamped from Salituri's having left his seventh Labatt's Blue unfinished.

Somewhat depressed by this exchange, I considered heading home, but then where would that be? Surely it was not the premium casket my corpse laid in. To hang about my parents' home would constitute something no less terrifying than a haunting. I thought to drop in on the post-funes reception of Big Rog, now taking place in the shoddy living room of Big Rog's uncle Dean, whom the town had taken to calling "Deaner" as an extension of their unironic admiration of the *FUBAR* protagonist.

Then she appeared, the star incarnate, looking at least 85% as beautiful as she had on that Monday, September 6 of 2003, not quite Margaret-tier, but a real accomplishment ten years down the road. She kicked snow off her own boots in the vestibule, then punched snow off the jackets of a few toddlers. I wrapped my wisps around her shoulders in some facsimile of an embrace.

Of course she wouldn't have brought toddlers to a funes where an OD'd corpse was not just present but the main event. And sure, maybe she was only at the PFR because her grandparents owned the reception hall. But as she said hello to my mother, as she sashayed her children amongst the cheek-pinching old Italian ladies, I constructed a narrative:

She had snuck off from her accountant husband, citing some toddlerian library event, but really to see me one last time, because Bob Stickman's account of my death had reminded her of the time we'd laughed about the Nicolet Tavern being her favourite tavern. She'd remembered how I'd marked her high school uniform shirt with my pen and then felt bad about it, how she'd pushed down my cuticles saying someone had to do it for me, and perhaps she'd remembered that love did not require eternal reciprocation to have meant something once.

My siblings were excused from school the next day. All afternoon Maisie seemed very bored. Her friends at school were texting with infuriating infrequency. She watched entire seasons of content on Netflix without really watching. Sometimes she'd be in the kitchen eating Bagel Bites while the content streamed on in her bedroom. Millions of dollars of production value; the (aspirational) creativity of a few dozen writers, cinematographers, and editors; a complex cultural product intended as art—all to be streamed 5 x 8 inches with the percipient literally out to lunch.

My observances of David were limited by his frequent masturbatory forays. It was not my place to judge, only to afford privacy. My initial inadvertent observation of this behaviour found David wearing the VR headset. I averted my figurative wraith eyes from this image within milliseconds, but something about that image really said to me: "The future is here and it is hell."

In the evening I followed David to a small gathering at a friend's house. They were playing *nWo Revenge* on a classic gaming emulator hooked up to the TV. These boys lacked the long-handled triad controller that signified N64 to that blessed generation raised on *Mario Kart, Bond* (as we called *Goldeneye*), and this very *Revenge*, which, indicative of its primacy in the wrestling game market, we called simply *Wrestling*.

David's character La Parka was laying out, subject to endless chair shots from the pockmarked kid named Allan. Allan's instinctual use of the furniture spoke of the violent opportunism that would take him places in Sault Sainte Marie. For his part, David was ecstatic in his prostration. Here was the core of the SSM comic sensibility: "I am being beaten by a chair and I cannot rise." David squirmed. He cursed the one true God and his known associates. He threatened the rectal well-being of Allan's mother. David, as I had once done, suffered to entertain. Perhaps, also like me, he was an enthusiast of Roland Barthes, who wrote, "Wrestling presents man's suffering with all the amplification of tragic masks . . . It is obvious, of course, that in wrestling reserve would be out of place, since it is opposed to the voluntary ostentation of the spectacle, to this Exhibition of Suffering which is the very aim of the fight. This is why all the actions which produce suffering are particularly spectacular, like the gesture of a conjuror who holds out his cards clearly to the public."

An e-cigarette appeared. The e-cigarette produced some digital correlative to the once-exclusively analog marijuana experience. This was disconcerting. Line-toeing and pseudo-athletic types such as old narrating Thomas Astaire here hadn't even considered weed until the final year of high school. More alarming was how second-nature it seemed to David's friends. There was no, "On Wednesday night we're going to get so baked and play *Wrestling*." They didn't congregate in some shed where some elaborate "buckets" setup made them all so catatonically high they'd have to avoid parents for the next calendar month or so. Just conservative little puffs on the laser pointer, like fifty-year-old men sitting in a garage talking about lesser-known Warren Zevon tracks such as *Werewolves of London.*

Of course it was Allan, with his acne and his well-timed chair shots, who removed a little blue Rexall prescription bottle from his pocket.

"Anyone want a perc?"

Another kid, the best looking among them, and *ergo* the most moralistic and decent, and so of course named Ryan, crinkled his eyebrows at Acne Allan and then sideways head tilted towards my brother, who noticed but did not acknowledge the offer or the tilt.

"Oh my bad," said A.A.

"Relax, they're just percs," said David. "My mom had them after her ankle thing. I took a few after my wisdom teeth were taken out."

His message was apparent. "No need to walk on perc-related eggshells around me, fellows. The death of my brother is wholly unrelated to whatever recreational opioid abuse we responsible drug-users might choose to partake in."

This was all Acne Allan needed to hear. Betraying the whole "innocent percs" routine, he expertly placed four percs in a smaller Ziplock bag he'd brought for this express purpose and crushed them up using the underside of a ceramic coin receptacle fabricated in the likeness of Nintendo's Luigi. He motioned the gamers over, collecting five dollars from each, excluding my brother, who was provided his lines *gratis*, due to my death, or Allan's self-awareness of his minor gaffe.

Glad to have been worth something, in the end.

A moment after David's line was snorted, his brows turned inwards, occupying the glabella area, as if he was thinking, "So this is what the fuss is about." I'd figured he was lying or confused about the wisdom teeth percs. Given the current prescription drug abuse climate in Pawateeg, he'd likely been given Tylenol 3s at the most.

A battle royal commenced with a heightened level of flow and camaraderie. Wins were now celebrated with ecstatic couch-jumping. The laughter came more frequently, which made sense, because as the aggressive/defeatist tenor had gone out of the jokes, they'd become funnier.

I felt like departing from the town. I checked on windbreaks at White River and Elliot Lake. All impenetrable. I wondered if this wasn't affecting the townspeople on some subconscious level. Was that why those who didn't leave for university at nineteen found it so hard to break these occulted boundary lines? Was that why the beautiful bartenders were so dispiriting to the man eating two poutines? Could he somehow intuit the magnetic pull drawing them out of his life, leaving nothing behind but the cheese curds?

I desired to make peace with my situation. If I was stuck here like the poutine man, I would do something he was incapable of. I would gain an understanding of the place. Our elementary school teachers had tried to foist the town's tepid history upon us, but it was no different than learning how photosynthesis worked, something you learned only to forget. Perhaps, in death, a deeper understanding of my hometown would make my confinement tolerable. More probable, it would be like a death row inmate learning the interior design history of his particular death row, bothering the guards for increasingly abstruse renderings, occasionally writing the design team to compliment them on their gift for evoking the godforsaken.

In this spirit of optimism, I flew to the Korah Library. Lacking the agency to pull a book from a shelf, necessity brought about an important discovery. There was no real size maximum or minimum to my wisp manifestation, so I could shrink myself down to the microscopic level, such that I might exist in between the pages of a book, and in this condition, though it was quite straining on my wraith eyes, I could read.

I consulted binders containing census details. The population stood at 73,000. This had declined less than I'd expected. Every class of high school seniors immediately left with about a 90% non-retention rate. Even the rigorous birthing schedules of your Adelle Salituris could not offset this. I had noticed an influx of Indian and Asian youth had been duped into attending Sault College and Algoma University, however. They'd been sold a verdant bill of goods, never told that Toronto was ten hours of nothing away. Or that the Sault was so geographically spread out that mere mall visiting would require an eighty-minute bus ride from their college residence.

In the archives I chanced upon one manuscript entitled *The Story of Baw-a-ting; being the annals of Sault Sainte Marie*, by Edward Henry Capp.

Capp introduces his work:

> Of the past of Sault Sainte Marie, its traditions, its love and hates, and its ever changing sons and daughters, we know somewhat and herein is set down in writing what love both ancient and modern has been collected. If in the perusal of these pages someone may be stirred to greater interest and better love for the town of his birth

or adoption, the work of gathering these notes will not
have been in vain.

When the Algonquin arrived, *they could press no further
westward for the time and back they refused to go.* Stuck even
then, but with the *magnificent supply of food in the abundant
fish of the rapids, they pitched their wigwams and settled down,
and Sault Sainte-Marie became their home.* No different than
the tow truck driver, or Rex with his crushed legs, or my
father, thinking: "I can survive here. I may not survive
elsewhere, heard those houses in Mississauga go for three-
quarters of a million, so this place must be good or at least
acceptable, eh."

I was already intending to finish the entire book in one
opiated sitting when I read the following:

> If the work is not as voluminous as some might wish it
> to be, it may perhaps serve as a skeleton to be clothed by
> a more perfect form of words by some writer of the future.

"It is my hope that you will be that writer," said the
Wraith of Sir Edward Henry Capp, then present inside his
book with me.

"Whoa," said I.

"Observe such words, fellow spectre, and tell me they
do not omen well," spoke the Wraith of Capp in a dignified
elocution. "Few have come to consult this volume. In fact,
less than few. In fact, you are the first! Ahh, no sense
bemoaning a limited readership, state of Canadian
publishing is it not? Alas, my writer of the future has come.
At last, a protégé!"

"Might have picked the wrong guy," I said. "Never really
refined my technique. Kind of all over the place. One

feedback that came up quite often in the *Onyx*-sponsored workshops was that my characters were nothing but salty caricatures."

"Are these opium-sniffing fools not worthy of some salinization?" asked the Wraith of Capp.

"Another reason I'm probably not the man for the job," I remarked, "is no hands to type."

"I'll teach you how to write physically, but also stylistically, if need be," spoke the Wraith of Capp. "As my worthy student, nay, as my worthy colleague, you will complete the story of Baw-a-ting. On many a pensive evening I've considered completing this history myself, yet, lo, I have lost touch with the vernacular."

I felt two conflicting emotions: I was inspired by Capp's lofty rhetoric, as well as his unfounded belief in me, but I also felt a sense of dread. I told myself the dread was related to the onerous task being prescribed me. But in my wraith heart I knew it for what it was, the onset of withdrawal.

As it was late, the Wraith of Capp suggested we commence my tutelage at the archives in the morning.

"Why not now?" I asked.

"I must rest."

"Wraiths rest?"

"Wraiths can," he said.

With a jittery feeling contraindicative of rest, I checked back in on the N64 party. When it ended I decided to follow the departing Acne Allan to get a sense of the Acne Allan experience. Nor was I the only one following him.

He walked two blocks, each step crunching down upon hard-pack snow, creating the vexatious sound I'd always loathed. Each crunch sent a shiver down my figurative spine, exacerbating the non-physical equivalent of the shakes I was starting to experience.

Acne Allan reached an address on Carol Court, paused in the driveway, typed peevishly into his phone, and eventually exhaled visibly into the -18°C night before knocking on the door.

An overweight kid roughly A.A.'s age answered the door.

"Hey man, what's going on?" asked Allan.

"Uh, just about to go to bed."

"Coo coo," said Acne Allan.

Coo coo, for *cool cool*, had been a frequently-employed neologism towards the end of my high school experience. I was disheartened to hear it living on in the lexicon of the Acne Allans of this era.

"Want to come in or something?" asked the fat kid.

"Guess so," said A.A.

"Want a pop?" asked the fat kid.

"Should look into the SodaStream," said A.A., "Nobody needs all that sugar."

The fat kid, looking a little hurt, cracked his own Coca-Cola Classic just as his father joined them in the kitchen.

A.A. gave the father the same peevish expression he'd worn while texting.

"Say, want to see some of my wood turnings, Allan?" asked the father.

"Oh boy, do I ever," said Allan.

Allan then provided the fat kid with an upwards head nod, the dismissive kind, to indicate, "Our time is done here pal. Go drink your syrup in peace."

In the wood-turning workshop, Allan affected a harsh tone. "C'mon Raphael, I walk all the way here in subarctic temperatures and you won't answer my texts? I've got to knock and pretend I'm friends with Damian for fifteen minutes."

"Sorry Allan," said Raphael, "I was in the shower."

"No need to get gussied up on my account," said A.A.

"Was washing diarrhea off my thighs, if you must know," said Raphael.

Allan rubbed contemplatively at the most carbuncular

region of his forehead.

"You're lucky I could get these," Allan continued. "Two 80s. They're going to be $120 each though."

"They were $100 last time," pleaded the incontinent wood-turning enthusiast.

"There's a shortage. I'll be honest, I paid $110 for these, and there needs to be what the business world refers to as a *markup*. Otherwise where's my ROI?"

"Tell you what," said Raphael, counting his wad of twenties, "I've got $200 here. How about you give me two and I throw in this baseball bat that I wood-turned myself. Took me three months."

"Own a nice metal Easton myself," said A.A., a tone of menace easing into his voice.

"Can't you quarter one?" asked Raphael. "Give me one pill and three quarters of another pill. I have a pill cutter right here under my chisels."

A.A. laughed the cruel laugh of the acne-afflicted. A laugh I'd laughed a time or two.

"You think I'm chopping this up, getting Oxy dust everywhere, leaving myself with some misshapen and undersized quarter that I can't even sell? I'm in a good mood, Raph. I'll take the $200, but you're going to owe me an extra $60 next time. Not $40. We're learning about this thing called *interest* in accounting. Lucky for you we don't get to compound interest until next week."

"Thank you. Thank you Allan," said Raph.

Raph halved a pill in his pill cutter and popped it into his mouth.

"Should give snorting a try," suggested Allan, "Quicker onset."

Allan left the place, kicked at some snow, and must have

been feeling so good about the customer base he was building that he failed to notice the all-too-apparent undercover police car trailing him from a block behind.

Bad Doug Bindi insufflated a key bump of cocaine and chuckled.

"You going to bust the kid now, Bad Doug?" asked a deputy.

"You're green, rookie. Green as goose shit."

En route to the Korah Library the next morning, I chanced across one area where the local economy was burgeoning: a film shoot. Compelled by a competitive Northern Ontario tax credit rather than any kind of local talent base, upstart producers from Toronto and Vancouver frequently shot their forgettable productions in Sault Sainte Marie. Accustomed to subsistence or parentally-financed living, these producers would use the credit to live high on the hog at the Water Tower Inn for a few weeks. Profitability never being more than a tertiary concern of the creditors, the Sault had landed productions as prestigious as *Lady Psycho Killer* and *Coconut Hero*. Like the comic books say: you don't get the *Coconut Hero* you want but rather the *Coconut Hero* you need.

Today's shoot, however, was a highly-coveted Local Production. It was a propaganda video for the nefarious Titans of Thor, the ersatz white supremacist group that patrolled the town under the guise of civic responsibility and criminal deterrence.

Based on the call sheet, I realized the Titans' promo video was a direct response to an Economic Development

Council-commissioned promo video titled *Come See What We See*. That video featured, *viz*, city hall; Point Des Chenes, with its infinitely unsatisfying pictographs; a bonfire—yes, come see that we have bonfires here; dirt biking; canoeing; paddle-boarding; regular biking; walking, even; a low-energy ultimate Frisbee game; snowboarding at Searchmont; a game of volleyball in the snow; skiing, also at Searchmont; snow biking, rather unappealingly; cross-country skiing, at Hiawatha this time; and then the fall colours at Hiawatha too, losing any sense of season-specific flow that might have structured this hodgepodge of shots; the 4506-metre International Bridge; a rare Sault clothier; an ice cream cone, as if those weren't available in every town; some lady sewing, same deal; RotaryFest, with all the glitz and glamour commonly associated with Rotary Clubs; the fair that comes to every town once a year; apples and spinach in a grocery store, we got those too; shopping bags in the station mall, indicative that commerce occurs here despite what you might have heard; the two Chinese food restaurants—hark, avail thyself of this culinary diaspora; some chic-looking bars long since closed; Sault College, widely considered one of the worst in all the land; and then that *pièce de resistance*, that obvious closer, that clarion call of inclusion and tolerance that should bid welcome to all comers: a Sikh student. Perhaps it was this Sikh student, minding his own business, wearing his Algoma U backpack but also his dastar, that inspired the Titans' own responsorial *viz*.

A local upstart director was shouting into an unnecessary bullhorn, directing the Titans to march about the library in formation for the "needle watch" sequence. Since there weren't any discarded needles nearby, a non-union propmaster scattered a dozen 6" low-dead-space syringes with permanently attached needles about the library steps, sharp-ends facing the camera.

Concerned and out-of-frame librarians looked on, as these needles created a hazard for patrons. The patrons had actually been, rather inconveniently for them, cordoned off behind some yellow emergency tape on the steps of the abutting OmniVoice Communications call centre. "They didn't even apply for a permit," whispered one librarian, but the librarians all knew the Titans had a handshake deal with Bad Doug and there was nothing to be done.

One of the few handsome Titans of Thor picked up a needle, placed it in a "sharps disposable" bag, looked into the camera, smiled, and gave the old thumbs up. "Okay, we got the shot," said the upstart.

For the next sequence, a man of indistinct-yet-swarthy racial composition made a play for an elderly woman's purse, though of course the woman and the racially-indistinct person were both Titans of Thor, and engaged in what only might generously be styled as *acting*. After a couple takes, the non-union makeup girl re-darkened the racially-indistinct man's complexion to the extent possible using her commercial-grade resources.

The Titans of Thor were filmed playing Frisbee, volleyball, walking, biking, almost frame for frame larceny from *Come See What We See,* the Titans' likely means of essaying, "We see the same things you see, *i.e.* biking, walking, *etc.*, but we also see a bunch of disgusting drug addicts needlin' up our library steps, and we can't help but notice the complexions of those accosting our elderly, so let's not disregard those sights entirely if we're talking about seeing what we see in Sault Sainte Marie."

The blondest available T.O.T. toddler ate from an ice cream cone. "Great stuff," said the upstart, no doubt eager to bank some less overtly fascistic imagery for his reel.

To show that the Titans were nothing like the white supremacist group that numerous publications had painted them as, a few reasonable Titans were shown breaking up a crudely-staged white supremacist rally, even though no full-blown white supremacist rallies were known to have taken place in Sault Sainte Marie since the 1920s, when they were known to have taken place all the time. An Allgemeine SS Officers Schirmutzen was slapped off a head, the dramatic effect of which was slightly mitigated when the victim and the hat-knocker broke out laughing in an inevitable iteration of their Titans of Thor camaraderie. A Luftwaffe-adorned lectern was kicked down. A copy of *Mein Kampf* was tossed into a garbage can. The upstart director couldn't quite get this shot on his SLR, requiring multiple takes. Finally T.O.T. Heinrich Von Driessen, owner of that copy of *Mein Kampf*, inquired if the commercial's budget would replace his second-edition copy of *Mein Kampf*, and if not, wouldn't it have been polite if some T.O.T. production type had mentioned the need for so many tosses, such a struggle, in which case Heinrich Von Driessen could have brought his trade paperback of *Mein Kampf* that he used for everyday reading and highlighting instead of his show copy that he kept under glass in his biergarten/Florida room.

In the Korah Library's archives I met Sir Edward Henry Capp. The archives were empty. I assumed the other archival researchers were still cordoned off on the OmniVoice steps, but over time I would realize that there were never any other archival researchers.

"Let's commence with your existing knowledge of this great land, *Baw-a-ting*, or *Pawateeg*, or as the Anishinabek preferred, *Bawitigong*, once called Sault du Gaston, known to you as Sault Sainte Marie, or often The Soo. Young man, what knowledge of your birthplace clings to your breast?" asked the Wraith of Edward.

"There's not a ton that clings to the old breast. I know Wayne Gretzky played for the Greyhounds. A lot of people talk about that. I know that Clergue guy started the steel plant and then stole all the money or something. I know somebody wrote that book *A Good Place to Come From*, but only because I used to see it on my grandma's book shelf, not because anyone ever talks about it. I know there's a bunch of Nazis outside right now."

"Hounds!" cried the Wraith of EHC, "And I don't mean the Greyhounds. I mean the colloquial expression of displeasure. What pity, what shame, that you, Thomas, know not of Longfellow's poem *Hiawatha*, which describes these very lands, that you know not the verses Rudyard Kipling provided us for the cenotaph, or the remark made by Ernest Hemingway: 'At the present time, the best rainbow trout fishing in the world is in the Rapids at the Canadian Soo.'"

"When was that present time exactly? With all due respect Capper . . . do you mind if I call you Capper? With all due respect Capper, that's not a whole lot in a two-hundred-year history of whatever. A couple notables pass through and send a postcard afterwards. Is that what you're giving me to work with here?"

Perhaps knowing from experience that immaterial wraith slaps posed no concussive consequence upon the victim, the Wraith of Capp only sighed and led me by the ear to the Clergue fonds in the archives.

"We start with Clergue . . . "

"Clergue, Clergue, Clergue," I said, as bored then by Clergue as I'd been preparing a grade seven presentation on him.

"Clergue! Clergue! Clergue!" shouted the Wraith of EHC, full of virility, a cheerleader for Clergue.

In the fonds Clergue walked above the frozen St. Mary's rapids, surveying all that might come to be. In the fonds Clergue harnessed the mighty rapids, founded the Lake Superior Power Company, tried to draw industrialists from the world over, failed, and so founded his own paper mill, and steel plant, and machine shop, all while being contemporaries with the likes of Andrew Carnegie and Thomas Edison.

"Okay, so this Clergue guy was impressive. Started the

whole thing in motion. But ever think maybe all these citizens, these fentanyl addicts and beer guzzlers, all these men who interfere with minors, ever think these people would be better off if Clergue had maybe just enjoyed the scenery, caught a couple walleye or whatever Hemingway was so worked up about, and been on his merry way? It was isolated then, it is isolated now. It's three hours to Sudbury, Capper. And Sudbury isn't exactly a hell of a town."

"What man, and I practise charity to name you as such, could possess so little loyalty to his birth soil?" asked the Wraith of EHC.

"I think TV changed all that," I said, taking on a sociological air. "You could watch the better places on TV, so no need to care about your own soil so much. Like how much Clergue can an audience be expected to absorb before simply tuning out, is what I'm asking now. We had Tiffani-Amber Thiessen to look at. We still do."

I could sense Cappinski was on the defensive, unsure of his life's work and personal haunting choices, so I went for the jugular.

"Is it fair to say, Sir Edward, that when Clergue brought about all that industrial progress, and the place pulsed with potential, the Soo peaked then and there, at the dawn of the twentieth century? And when none of the industrialists came, Fred Clergue left just enough industry behind, the still-extant steel plant and the still-extant mill, so that the place was left to fester on, like a stage two cancer patient whose cancer never metastasizes, but just cancers on forever."

"Good Thomas, opium was widely available in my time, though I was morally hygienic enough to stay well clear. I will credit your malignity to the poppy and to the devil. I will take some air. Please do read on. And please do affect a more respectful tone upon my return. If this is not possible, I fear this acquaintance, an acquaintance I have waited upon for a century and many months more, will come to an abrupt end."

One aspect of withdrawals, in my experience, was an exponential increase in my tendency towards cruelty. I understood that I was taking all of my death regrets and all of my life regrets out on Edward H. Capp, and by extension, on the Sault, because I had no one else to talk to, no one else whom it would be satisfying to hurt.

An introduction to a speech Clergue had delivered to the Toronto Board of Trade supported my thesis. I wordlessly presented it to the Wraith of Edward Henry Capp upon his return from taking air.

> I am a back-woodsman from the wilds of Algoma, but I have a sufficient sense of civilization about me to appre-ciate very fully the compliment you have paid me in inviting me to address you on this subject. I suppose that the gentlemen here, like those throughout the most of Southern Ontario with whom I have come in contact, view Algoma—which, of course, includes the most of Northern Ontario—as an unknown country; or rather known principally and almost only for its barren and deserted appearance. So barren and deserted is that appearance that even the Canadian Pacific times its trains so as to pass through that territory at night, in order not to offend the gaze of its passengers with the unpropitious aspect. That was the way Algoma looked to me; that was the way that part of Ontario presented itself to me when I first came to this country.

"Sounds like he's presenting the opposing view so he can flip the script and say how cool all us Saultites are, right?

But he never does. He just cuts a promo about how he turned this unpropitious dump into a cradle of industry. As a representative of northern Ontario, he's so self-effacing. He knows his role, like The Rock used to say. He knows he's describing a place that his audience is indifferent towards. I can't tell you how many times I've told other Torontonians I was from the Soo, and even though it's just an eight-hour drive, they had not heard of the place, thought maybe it was near Parry Sound."

The Wraith of Edward directed himself to an archive chair and crossed his leg wisps.

"Got time for one more? So the citizens of Sault Sainte Marie throw Clorg a banquet in 1901 because of all he's done for the community, and this is how he kicks that speech off—"

> When the industrial undertakings, which have so far progressed in your midst, were first projected six years ago, we found Sault Sainte Marie a small village far removed from the centers of commercial and industrial activity in Canada, comprising a total population of not over 2,500, the majority of whom, and I mean this as a compliment, were people of disappointed ambitions.

"He meant it as a compliment," I continued. "'People of disappointed ambitions.' Amazing how the character of a people can transcend history, isn't it? Check the ledger at the Butter Chicken Factory in a few months and you'll find the disappointed ambitions Clark knew. Go to the *Halloween Store!*'s financiers today and dare to ask a question as innocuous as, 'So, how's business?'"

"For a man wholly lacking in academic bona fides, you've mastered the art of robbing from context like a craven highwayman to illustrate whichever specious argument best suits your particular pathology, Thomas; and so perhaps my faith in you is not ill-founded," said Capp. "Nevertheless, this exchange has wearied me, and though an hour remains before luncheon, again I must rest. I'll leave you with these words, Longfellow's, which may sooth all that aches in you, all that makes you hate the place you come from, for the sole reason that you hate your own self."

> On the shores of Gitche Gumee,
> Of the shining Big-Sea-Water,

so began Longfellow's long poem about some Ojibwe battle that was a big snooze so I won't reproduce it in these pages. After briefly wondering what kind of luncheon Capp was talking about, I decamped from the library archives with the intention of letting the Wraith of Edward Henry Capp walk the Korah Library's hallways in solitude, thinking about his boyfriend Clergue for eternity, haunting and bloviating and forever fumigating the historical relics of a place divorced from history.

My bed had been made by my mother. Who could ever sleep in it again but me? I fixed my non-localized tendrils between the bedspread and the crisp yellow sheets. I tried to rest the approximation of my head upon a pillow. Through some small miracle, the kind that sometimes affects the withdrawing or the Sault Sainte Marie-situated, I fell asleep.

I was awoken by two visiting parties: the Wraith of Big Rog and the Wraith of dead Mellissa Gladstone.

"Nice to see you two getting acquainted," I said.

"Tom, I'd like to tell you something," said Rog, a bit of a hitch in his voice, "Mellissa and I have decided to live as one."

"One what?"

"One ghost I guess."

"Rog, I hardly think . . . "

As those of a Big Rogian bent are wont to sputter, he said, "The ghost of Steve Bortolucci is living as one with the ghost of Matt Scornianki, and th-they're not even gay. It's like a comfort thing."

What could be done? There was no ethical council of

wraiths to whom I could report Big Rog. Here I was practising your textbook Sault Sainte Marie abdication of moral responsibility. Certainly Rog was not the first of his persuasion in Paw-a-teeg to be negligently ignored. Predating the Oxy epidemic was another unwholesome pastime in Bawitigong: pederasty! During Ken DeLuca's twenty-year reign of terror at the Catholic District School Board (1972 to 1993), female students would weary of his flirting, of his kissing of their breasts, of his "odiousness." Female students would complain to their parents. They'd throw eggs at his truck. They'd attempt suicide. "'Kenny" being a key infield cog of his softball nine, a second baseman cop might warn a troublemaker to complain less frequently about the kissing of her breasts. A back-catching priest could address Deluca's classrooms regarding the perniciousness of lies. Ken's brother was a trustee of the school board. When the complaints reached a head Ken was transferred, four times in all, including once to an all-girls school where girls changed out of their gym uniforms in the hallway, and where his wife taught.

Nearly half the Catholic District School Board's administrators were implicated, if never actively punished, when the many pelvic grindings and breast caresses suffered by Ken DeLuca's female students finally came to light, and as Barthes wrote in the wrestling essay, "A light without shadow elaborates an emotion without secrets."

In his *Globe and Mail* article of September 21, 1996, "21 Years of Wickedness," Michael Valpy argues:

> It is outside belief that, for more than 20 years, there was a conspiracy by principals and senior board officials to protect Mr. DeLuca and, indeed, create an environment in which he could abuse his students. The credible

explanation is that an authoritarian, hierarchical, religious
school board considered itself too morally superior to be
harbouring someone like Ken DeLuca."

Kenny spent four months in Millhaven Institution
lifting weights. He was physically and spiritually hearty
upon his return to Ba-wa-teeg. He was as proficient at
softball as ever, even hit with a little more pop in his bat.
Meeting friends on the boardwalk, he was all "hale fellow
and well met." He often exceeded the boundaries of his
parole to go fishing. Should a parent with murder in their
eyes blare a car horn at him outside the YMCA, Kenny
would throw his palms out in the well-known "ease up"
gesture. In short, he was acting like a real Bow-it-ig-o-win-
in, a *Sault Sainte Marie man.*

"It's what I want," pleaded Mellissa, the tone of
desperate love in her voice illustrating why it was always
exploitive for a man to romance a girl.

I should have righteously floated away from Big Rog
there and then, but I'd known Big Rog since we were
children, and as the outsider Michael Valpy described it,
the Sault *is a portrait of a working-class, largely Italian-
Canadian community whose members accepted the advice of
their priest and other authority figures and whose adult males
—fathers, educators, policemen, politicians—grew up together,
socialized together, played sports together.* Valpy must have
consulted that choropleth map. He understood we were
stuck in the middle of precisely nowhere, together, and so
we'd cover up each other's reckless fentanyl cuts, our
drunken manslaughters, our sex crimes, all that should be
rightly alleged against us by our victims. What Valpy
wondered was why didn't this loyalty ever extend to them,
to our victims?

"We're so happy to have your blessing," said the fused Wraith of Mellissa/Big Rog, though I had offered no blessing. "What have you been up to?"

"Learning things you just wouldn't believe about Francis H. Clergue," I said, this weak jest serving as the actual blessing.

"How come?"

"Great question that I couldn't begin to answer. But hey, did you know that in 1922 they made a silent movie about Francis H. Clergue and his mastery of the St. Mary's Rapids. Starring Mary Astor."

"Did not know that, no," said Rog, "Not sure if I cared to."

"It was more like a series of slides than a movie . . . "

Big Rog, the consummate guilty party, interrupted, "I mean, sure, Mellissa likes to see what her friends are up to, so naturally I accompany her, but I am totally not doing this for the reasons that got me in trouble before. It's just being a good boyfriend. You may have noticed we don't feel that way anymore."

"I had noticed that, Rog, yes. Nearby impossible for a wraith to experience lust, only the longing that is the saddest part of lust. What a bargain this death is."

"And we go to the dragon parties," added Mellissa.

I expressed my keen interest in hearing more about these dragon parties.

"Come on, we'll show you."

We flew to one of Sault Sainte Marie's many Clergue-era houses in Jamestown, now given over to water damage and dry rot, and best described as a drug den or flophouse.

Three hungry men were huddled around a piece of foil, a barbecue lighter, and a straw. I never quite understood dragon chasing. Why so small of a straw? Wouldn't a personal-sized funnel guarantee 100% transmittance of the smoke into one's lungs? This may explain the prolonged appeal of oral opiate abuse for so many raging addicts. You put the pill in your mouth, it digests in the stomach, passes through the liver—waste is impossible.

"Watch this," said the Wraith of Big Rog.

Their enjoined presence flitted in amongst the smoke, intervening between the tinfoil and the low-efficiency straws of the hungry men.

"Do you get high from that?" I asked.

"I think so. I think we do."

On the next hit I intermingled with the smoke. As an armchair student of (and *ergo* slightly less susceptible to) the placebo effect, I knew I felt nothing.

"Did you feel it? Did you get a little high? Not like the old times but something?" asked Big Rog.

"I did. I feel great right now," I lied.

"I know! Me too!" said the Wraith of Rog.

"You said we could go see the girls," spoke the Wraith of Mellissa, "They're at the restaurant now. They're probably almost done."

"Want to come to Boston Pizza, Tom?" asked Rog.

"It's what we do, isn't it? As Saultites? We chase dragons and eat overpriced appetizers."

At Boston Pizza my sister Maisie was sitting at a booth with her friends Jay and Andie. They were ordering the $12 milkshakes meant for the young, the young at heart, and the glucose-dependent. Maisie ordered a Smartie Supreme. Jay ordered a virgin Pina Colada. Andie, somewhat hefty as she was, only ordered a second 320-millilitre bottle of Perrier.

Jay hunched and whispered to the table, "Oh my God, I think they put alcohol in this."

"Let me try it," said Maisie, already slurping viscous liquid up through her Nestle-branded Smartie Supreme straw.

"Oh jeez, I think you're right," she said.

Fearing the Colada's calories yet needing to contribute to the illicit goings-on, Andie asked, "Where are we going to get alcohol for the dance, you guys?"

"I can ask Darby Scarborough to get us some," said Jay.

"He's so gross," said Maisie.

The Wraith of Mellissa, who'd later confide to always having carried a torch for Darby Scarborough, affected a huffing noise.

"He has a fake ID though," said Jay.

"There's another option," said Andie, sipping dissatisfied from her Perrier, "My dad gets these pills . . . "

Like Acne Allan before her, Andie sensed she'd made a faux pas relative to my fentanyl overdose and resultant death, causing her to reassure the table, "Not the ones that your brother did though, sorry. Just like wisdom teeth pain ones. Sorry."

"Do they feel like alcohol?" slurred Jay, though all we assembled wraiths had seen the bartender prepare her sugar colada with nary a drop of rum.

"They feel better than alcohol. They feel like a hug from the inside," said Andie, "Perfect for a dance. Can you just imagine Darren Steen wrapping his arms around you when you're already being hugged from the inside?"

"How many can you get?" asked Maisie.

Did she need a hug from the inside because of my brief and traumatic imposition upon her life? Or did she just want one for the reasons everyone wants a hug from the inside?

"My dad buys like fifty a week for his knee or something. He actually gets them from the drugstore and then he gets more from some delivery boy because the drugstore has inconvenient hours he says. I'm sure he won't notice a few missing. He's always losing his memory and acting crazy 'cause he's old."

"Get six," said Jay, "Then we'll have two each. One for before the dance and one around midnight when things get steamy."

Seated by the bar, not ten feet from the girls' booth, close enough to spit into Maisie's Smartie Supreme had he been inclined, which he probably was, listening in, cataloging clues, three shots of tequila before him, handy cocaine-bumping key confidently laid out right beside the leftmost shot glass, cocaine residue in the key's ridges, practically challenging the manager to ask him to pocket the cocaine-encrusted key, sat based Bad Douglas Bindi, anti-heroic wraith of the pages to follow.

I was looking to cleanse the palate after all these foreshadows of doom. At home I found that it was my mother's night out with Margaret. When Margaret's BMW pulled into the driveway I decided to tag along, out of a desire to reconnect with my mother, sure, but also out of an enthusiasm for Margaret's ongoing winsomeness.

Avenues of conversation having been exhausted at the workplace, they clicked tongues over the scourge of heartworm. The comportment of their poorer and obviously Oxy-dependent clientele base was discussed.

"One hundred and ten dollars," Margaret kept repeating in disbelief.

The gist was some molecule-dependent party wouldn't pay $110 for lifesaving medication to keep his beloved and only four-years-old miniature poodle from an encroaching, swift, and painful death. He was opting instead to "let this thing play out," leading Margaret to provide the lifesaving medication *pro bono* after shaming the man for several minutes.

The two women fell into a silence lasting the entire span of the International Bridge. That might sound like a long silence, but that's only because of the puffery involved in the naming of this meagre four-kilometer bridge. Sault Sainte Marie, Michigan was close enough that it didn't interfere with my windbreak confinement. Yet young Saultites can't wait to turn twenty-one to visit the U.S. bars. Inferior by every possible bar quality metric, their appeal stems from their brief unattainability. You'd waited desperately to visit the Princess or the Butter Chicken Factory, but a month after your nineteenth birthday you realized those places weren't Studio 54 after all, but thank god there's something on the horizon, across the 4,600-metre bridge, which you could just run across if you wanted to, and you would cross that bridge one day and things would be fun, just as Margaret and my mother would visit the casino for fun, and things might be better, and if not better, different, and if not different, then at least some time will have been killed.

At the Kewadin Casino there was the standard slot clamour unworthy of description in this document, given that Capp, as editorial assistant, editorial intern more like, is urging brevity wherever possible. Margaret raised her eyebrows at my mother, a prompt for enthusiasm, *i.e.,* "Could it get any more distracting than this?"

Certainly it did not take much to please my mother. She had grown up on a farm in the town of Ophir, population ranging between a dozen or two dozen, depending on who was passing through town. Horses and buggies occupied the dirt roads more frequently than cars. Cows yielded milk and cream. Her family pickled and preserved. They skimmed the cream off the top of milk vats. There was maple candy in April. My mom was allergic to animals and spent most of her childhood in hospitals. Her father died from cancer when she was eight. She'd hid behind a wood-burning stove during the post-funes reception, not wanting to field the queries of "How are you doing?"—post-funes banter doing more harm than good even in those heartier times, it would seem. With no man to till the fields, farming became untenable. They planted Christmas trees one season but hardships made it impossible for them to harvest and sell them, so their 300 acres returned to forest. They moved from Ophir to Sault Sainte Marie, where my grandmother worked her way up from charwoman to cafeteria lady to respected baker. My mother was ashamed to bring friends back to their Gore Street apartment, but never wanted to let my grandmother realize that. This fragility had stayed with her, somehow, and as Capp once wrote of the fur trader John Johnston, *a cloud seemed to have rested on [her] youthful days, a shadow which was always a mystery to [her] hosts of friends, and which [she] never ceased to allude to with regret.* They scrimped and saved. Things improved once my aunt and mother were able to work. My mom became a receptionist. Soon they could afford a small television. They watched the movies denied to them in Ophir. *The Bridge on the River Kwai. Some Like It Hot.* Once so far out of reach, this level of comfort was enough consolation for her. She'd never need an opioid to enjoy the latest localized take on *Crime Scene Investigator P.I.* (e.g. *Crime Scene Investigator P.I., Phoenix*). All she'd need was a reasonable snack. When she married my father she was baptized as a Catholic and took Christ's charitable message to heart, spending her free time volunteering with the infirm and elderly, bringing them meals and keeping them company as she kept my grandmother company during a prolonged decline from Alzheimer's. Who would question such a life? This person whose dander allergies had hospitalized her for months of her childhood, who'd grown up on way too many potato-centric meals, who couldn't bring friends around Gore Street. All she'd wanted was our Sault Sainte Marie life, with its middle-class pleasantries, the D'Alessandro bread instead of the generic kind, the Tostitos and layered dips, the basement with its napkin couch and its cable television. The life I'd resented because I'd for some reason felt entitled to the sublime.

Now a part of all that comfort, namely me, was gone, but she had endured worse, and kept her head up then. Life was hard. It hadn't always been opiates. It had been all the variations of the devil: crib death, milk sickness for her forebearers even, or just mundane poverty, and then that lost father like all our lost love.

"I've got a fun idea for next month also," continued Margaret, "I saw in the *Sault Star* that they're doing a flash mob for opiate awareness."

"What's a flash mob?" asked my mom.

"You know like in the viral videos? Everyone is just sitting in the mall and then suddenly all the people in on the flash mob start dancing to the same song. And it blows everyone's mind."

"If they're advertising it, won't it be less mind-blowing?" my mom asked.

Margaret gave her an admonishing smile, an "aren't-you-wicked," but also a "no need to be negative about the apparent idiocy of the flash mob when they're trying their best" smile.

"It will be good for awareness," Margaret said.

That was the ultimate distraction if you were altruistic in Sault Sainte Marie and would not crush up a single

OxyContin 80, would not diddle even a distant acquaintance of your stepdaughter—you raised awareness for the more tangible issues in life: cancer, heart and stroke, opiate overdosing issues.

I was getting a little bored, about to fly back across the St. Mary's River to my bed, when I detected a distinct aura around me.

"Ah, the monozygotic brethren of our home and native land, Chippewa county, Chippewa being merely another of the red man's words for *Ojibwe*, our great enemies throughout the War of 1812 and beyond, our friends in commerce since—Sault Sainte Marie, Michigan!"

"Edward, how are things?" I asked.

"Not finding you at the archives was worrying," said the Wraith of EHC, "Now I meet you on an evening of field research. Well done you ripe stinker!"

"Yeah, actually just following people I know because what else am I supposed to do?"

A mild bristling from the Wraith of Capp's wisps.

"What else are you supposed to do? When you have yet to study the history of good John Curran, founder of the venerable *Sault Star*, the ultimate chronicler of Clergue's . . . "

"Hey, not to be presumptuous, but do come clean if you and Clerb, who was a—and here I'm quoting a variety of sources—'confirmed bachelor,' if you and Clerb had some kind of secret and homosexual love affair? Times have really changed regarding tolerance and accommodation and even outright celebration of these matters."

Capp affected a pacing motion, storming up and down the aisle that separated the Ellen slot machines from the Misty 50 slot machines. "Young sir, I was rector of the St. Luke's Cathedral and Chaplain of the 97th Regiment."

"Ya, ya, ya, ya, ya, ya, ya, ya, ya," I said.

After having spent the day at dragon chasing parties and Smartie Supreme parties, I figured a sense of duty might distract me from withdrawals and boredom.

"Just roasting you, Capp," I said, "I'm in."

"In what?"

"In on updating your history of Stink Sainte Marie."

"All to the mustard!" exclaimed Capp in such a way that I intuited *All to the mustard* must have meant *Oh good.* "Even if you care not for Clergue, you can record the ongoing history, the history of the now."

"Would love to, Capper, problem is, the history is a little hard to find. Vegas Kewadin profits stable as general economy declines. Overpriced sugar cocktails still popular at franchise restaurants. Dragon chasing in Jamestown living rooms now the norm rather than the exception."

"Why ever had this not occurred to me?" Capp laughed. "Here emerges the providential insight I'd always sought from a protégé."

"I prefer the title of managing editor, but do continue."

"Mark your own words, tutee. Why, it's the dragon of course. This mythical lizard our kinsmen chase so eagerly, so desperately, to the eternal recurrence of their sorrow. This will be our literal dragon. First we learn of its birth. Then we find the means of slaying it."

"Dragon was birthed by big pharma, Purdue I think. Purdue has nothing to do with the town."

"Akin to arguing the actions of Champlain had nothing to do with the pioneering spirit of Ermatinger," said the Wraith of Capp, laughing rather too heartily. "We start researching the dragon's birth bright and early tomorrow morning!"

"This is the battle you want to fight?" I asked. "First thing that's got your dander up in over a hundred years are some New York-based pain pill manufacturers?"

"Look around you," said Capp, "at the deviants who slumber on the library steps, at the defeat in the eyes of the food bank volunteer. This dragon is the only foe with the strength to fully and finally sink Sault Sainte Marie."

"Well, how about noon," I said.

"Noontide it shall be," said the Wraith of Capp agreeably. "Care to fly back to Baw-a-ting with me?"

"Just call it the Soo."

"Sooward ho!"

Our route home was diverted.

"Where are we going?" I asked.

"As many restful hours await us until forenoon, I wish to show you an important figure who verily keeps Ba-wa-teeg afloat. A vision to offset all the negativity you choose to mire yourself in."

I was brought to another grey-walled building that resembled a high school, the Ministry of Natural Resources outpost along St. Mary's River Drive. There we found the offices of the Sault Sainte Marie Anti-Erosion Task Force, where a wall of monitors displayed all manner of erosive outputs.

"Good Graeme Abbot monitors the erosion surrounding

the St. Mary's River each night from the hours of midnight to nine, at which time he finds himself replaced by good Michael Mount, whose efforts are of no less courage."

"Why is good Graeme sleeping?" I asked.

"Shift work causes all manner of nervous prostration, metabolic imbalance, the St. Vitus dance you're witnessing now, perhaps better known as jerking awake momentarily."

"I am noticing the St. Vitus dance," I said, "Maybe it has to do with that crushed pile of OxyContin 40s and that rolled-up twenty that Graeme is snoring beside."

"I would very much doubt so vile an accusation."

"Does that onscreen output reading 'Action Required' warrant concern?" I asked.

"Graeme Abbot will come to that in time," said the Wraith of Capp, clearing his throat, suddenly anxious to decamp from the Anti-Erosion Task Force's offices.

At my parents' home I found Acne Allan knocking at the door.

"Little late isn't it?" asked my father.

"Just dropping off *Astrobot*."

Acne Allan patted his backpack but produced no *Astrobot*. My father didn't understand that all of David's games were downloaded from the PlayStation Store and non-lendable. My brother slid across the linoleum kitchen floor in his socks to greet Allan in the foyer. What a thing it was—to execute a floor slide with such boyish grace even before opiates had entered one's system.

"I know you asked for five," said Allan in my brother's bedroom, "Here's six. Same price. First time bonus. And as a tribute to your brother, uh, God rest his eternal soul."

Allan crossed himself.

This was no mourner's solidarity. Allen was using the same strategy the Xalisco boys used to spread black tar heroin throughout the American heartland. He was coveting the economic value of a nascent junkie.

"Thanks bud," said my brother, "Should last me a while. I only really need to take like a quarter before the next *COD* regionals. Just to calm the nerves. I tighten up."

"I know that feel," responded Allan, "I've spent my whole life feeling tight."

Did this tight feeling cause the acne? Allan's insides were so coiled, so churning with dyspepsia that the only release was through the pores, but slowly, creating the bilious carbuncles that would only after weeks and months of agony burst through the epidermal threshold with torrents of blood and bile and pus. First the dark black blood, then red with an olive oil texture, until finally clear grease speckled hundreds of Kleenex from forenoon 'til come gloaming (as *gloaming* is obviously a word choice I'd make and not the editorial heavy-handedness of the Wraith of Capp interfering here)—and all in front of the mirror, mind you, all in the bright shame of the mirror. Who among us wouldn't want half a 40mg Oxycodone Hydrochloride Controlled-Release tablet after all that?

"I'd take one now," said my brother, "But I've got to get to sleep."

"Oh man, they are perfect for sleep," said Allan. "You'll never have a better sleep."

"Sounds like they're good for just about everything," said David, producing a pair of scissors.

Allan laughed as an experienced angler might at a young son's well-intentioned but ultimately-bungled lure choice.

"I'll quarter these for you," said Allan, getting out the same pill cutter I'd owned, the Apex Ultra Pill Splitter: $20 at Shopper's Drug Mart, $10 at Amazon.ca.

"Best investment you'll ever make," said Allan.

My father knocked on the bedroom door, leading to a great deal of scrambling to hide all the quartered pills beneath a pillow.

"Albert, your dad's waiting for you outside. I'm sure he wants to get home to bed."

Allan's father could wait in no car, having lost his license after a series of mid-intersection nod-offs. Allan's dad, not hearty of liver, his septum more or less a thing of the past, aversive to needles, perhaps in agreement with me about dragon chasing wastes—was at that very moment reading up on *boofing* procedures on r/opiates.com. I know this because I went and checked. I told you, milliseconds; all light-speed wraith transportation with nowhere to go.

The man waiting in the car outside was the intra-nasal cocaine addict, weapon of God's hard justice, and all-purpose hate machine, Sergeant Bad Doug Bindi, as astute readers may already have intuited.

I slept fitfully and dreamt (and yes, wraiths dream) of all the Bindian and erosive doom sure to befall my kinsmen.

Waking as shaky and depressed as I'd been since death, there was no relief on the horizon, not even the nociceptive hug of a shower I'd relied on prior to my awareness of opiates. With no better plans, I made good on my promise to the Wraith of Edward Henry Capp and arrived at the Korah Public Library shortly after noontide.

"More than a few quarter-hours late, you skunk. No matter, your absence has given me time to collate that material most pertinent to the dragon's slaying."

Capp started me off with the concise and bullet-pointed "A Brief, Blood Boiling History of the Opioid Epidemic" from *Mother Jones*.

Mother Jones—being an online publication—begged the question, "How?" Did wraiths have printing privileges I'd not been made aware of?

"How do you get on the Internet?" I asked him. "How did you print this? Do you have corporeal fingers hidden away in some wisp pocket?"

"Set to work, Thomas, and I may show you yet. Idle

much longer and cast your lot with the Archfiend."

Thus motivated, I moved on to the print-based, and significantly meatier, "Insys Founder Charged in Bribe Scheme Linked to Fentanyl-Based Painkiller" in the *New York Times*.

"That founder was John Kapoor," I said. "I was killed by John Kapoor. John Kapoor was giving press conferences saying he was making the world's craziest fuckin' super opiate because he felt sad about his wife's breast cancer, when really he just wanted billions of dollars. I always knew it was something like this, but the specifics are rather irksome."

"The brigand Kapoor wasn't alone!"

He directed me to the longest long-read yet, more non-fiction novel than magazine feature, "The Family that Built an Empire of Pain," in the *New Yorker*. I learned of Arthur and Mortimer Sackler, the medical marketing men who became wealthy on the backs of Valium and other tranquilizers in the 60s, but for whom wealth was not enough, and so they set the whole OxyContin train a-rollin' in the 90s with a downright fiendish campaign to convince doctors that pain was unacceptable and that OxyContin was not addictive (when they knew it was), and whose progeny's names now bloodied the walls of the world's most prestigious art galleries and various wings at Yale.

"While all deeply troubling, what's to be done?" I asked. "No history of the Soo can be a history of the Sacklers or John Kapoor. Our history is independent from them. And their history is transcendent. They imposed history on all of West Virginia, all of the middle American suburbs too. Even on the cartel's balance sheet."

The Wraith of Capp puffed himself up. He was going

in for the hard sell.

"We drive the history forward and stamp the name Baw-a-ting upon it. You and I boy, we bring the pestilence of Sault Sainte Marie to the doorstep of Kapoor, to the Sackler descendant with millions in the bank who prefers to identify as a—" the Wraith of EHC made a little expression of disgust—"singer-songwriter."

"Our confinement here restricts us from any Sackler-related agency," I said.

The Wraith of Capp pointed a wraith finger in the air. "The hour has come to explain my printing process, as well as my entrée into the World Wide Web."

"Just call it the Internet," I said.

We flew to the Sault Area Hospital's mental health unit, subatomically and specifically into the file cabinet of a Dr. Marlene Purvis, Clinical Psychiatrist.

"Gathered in these documents you'll find our subjects," said the Wraith of Capp.

I perused the case files of Purvis' schizophrenic patients.

"Young John Doan here printed that *Mother Jones* article and left it in the printer tray for us," continued Capp. "At some emotional cost to him, mind you, considering the snickering he endured from the Korah Library's insufferable archivist, which archivist spends little more than an hour a week writing that blog for the *Northern Hoot* and has done no real archival work in . . . ."

"Let's momentarily table the archival griping," I said, "Care to explain how these schizophrenics relate to the Sacklers and Kapoor?"

"Here are minds open to influence, Thomas. Here are our agents in the fleshly realm. Free from all barriers. Free to assault the Sacklers at will."

"Continue."

"We will haunt the dreams of John Doan and Patrick Gass and Amy Orlando and Jill Gertz. Fortuitously, these youths dream in the day as at night. We may well have to fend off competing wraiths eager to convey their own messages. As a man of the cloth, thus seasoned in the metaphysical realm, I've developed a knack for coming through the loudest and clearest."

"Great, we've got Jittery John Doan here spouting crazy nonsense about Sacklers," I said. "I can just feel the history living and breathing in Bawitigong again."

"These individuals are young and without criminal records, each medicated and living with family. Free to travel as they might. Using your understanding of the World Wide Web, Internet Explorer if you prefer the contemporary nomenclature, we instruct them to buy airline tickets. If we can't bring the Sacklers to our gallows, let us direct the hangman to them!"

"Rhetoric altogether more murderous than I'd expect from a Rektor in good standing," I said.

"Mere analogy. Our charges will only defile the Sackler holdings with aerosol'd paints. Upon a Sackler's doorstep, John Doan will spray-paint, 'OxyContin is killing Sault Sainte Marie.' A Kapoor-owned estate will be condemned by the words, 'Fentanyl has ruined the fine and good town of Sault Sainte Marie.'"

"Last one might be a little wordy," I said.

I would admit though, for a 161-year-old Clerguean history wonk, the Wraith of Edward Henry Capp had come up with a plan that might make the world take notice, might make history live again in Baw-a-ting.

First we visited the home of Patrick Gass, hereafter referred to as "the Brapster" based on the nickname 4chan's /lit board had given to the great maximalist novelist William H. Gass. The Wraith of Capp neither having even read *The Tunnel* nor being fond of fart humour, insisted upon the use of Patrick's Christian name in this document. Usage of "the Brapster" remains, however, a hill I am willing to die on.

EHC showed me the drill. As we'd shrunk ourselves down to enter a book, we shrank ourselves down to enter a brain. We penetrated a myelin sheath and cruised past parietal lobes and nodes of Ranvier, through the thalamus, back and forth, from axon terminals to dendrites, clearing a path. Through sheer force of motion we exorcised many screaming demons and angels asserting their salient concerns of apocalypse, of Jesus Christ's imminent return, of mind-control poisons in the drinking water. With the Brapster's consciousness clear, we delivered our message. My duty was to facilitate the booking of an airline ticket, the sneaking away from his family home at an opportune time, *etc*. I also got the Gass-man up to speed on New York City subway routes and how to find the home of Michael

Sackler-Berner, the "singer-songwriter," whom Capp loathed the most.

"A fine day's work," said Capp.

"Say, Capp, uh, Sir Edward, you'd mentioned this mind influencing trick is easier with schizophrenics, but is it possible with neurodivergent persons of all stripe? Autistics say? The OCD-afflicted? Plenty of those about."

"To an extent," said Capp, before changing the subject. "Shall we begin a new routine? A matutinal stroll around the grounds of Bellevue Park come dawntide?"

"Matutinal strolls sound good going forward," I remarked. "But next dawntide I've got plans."

The following forenoon I tested my own dream-haunting power by orchestrating a rib on the Wraith of Edward Henry Capp. I traversed the synapses of Jill Gertz and instructed her to print the following *Soo Today* news story, dated January 18, 2018, at the Korah Library where Capp was sure to see it in the morning.

Sault ranks in bottom five for young adults, study says

A bit of not-so-flattering news for Sault Sainte Marie from Point2 Homes News, a Saskatoon-based website which covers real estate market trends and news.

In a new study, Point2 Homes states the Sault ranks fifth in the five "Least Tempting Millennial Cities."

. . . The study wrote the Sault has the sixth most affordable housing market in Canada, but also has the third highest unemployment rate in the cities surveyed, noting the community already has a "low percentage of millennials already living in the city."

I then instructed Jill to type up and append the following

comic list to heighten the zestiness of the rib's effects:

The 3 Runners-Up
3) Fentanyl-Ville
2) Fireton
1) Sudbury

Confident in my oneirophaegic powers, I set about the day's real business. The classrooms at St. Patrick's were just as I remembered them. The carpets were either beige or purple. Who could know for certain after they'd been vacuumed ten million times? They had been steam-cleaned once or twice at the Ministry's behest. St. Patrick's was the lone survivor of a construction boom during the town's last-ever baby boom. Now Sister Mary Clare, St. Thomas, and St. Francis all sat empty, or housed old easels, or were in rare cases repurposed as *Halloween Stores!*

Adelle stood before the class, tired but benevolent, having little to give but giving it all away anyway. She read a Newbery Medal-winning novel to her grade seven class. These embossed silver metals always warned children of the boredom to come. There'd be character development, and denouement, and theme identification, though the theme was invariably *man versus nature*. All I'd ever wanted as a young reader was Christopher Pike, who disregarded YA conventions by writing extensively about tits. Tits! How we loved to read of them. We cared not for wolves, girls who rescued baby blue jays, or boys who survived and inevitably thrived on stupid Ship's Hull Ridge.

Adelle wore a tweed skirt with black leggings beneath it. The height of conservatism, but what love it must have engendered in those grade seven boys. Here she was with the small mole still above the leftmost crescent of her lip. The exasperated smile that seemed to say, "Oh come on." The lips sucked back from the gleaming white teeth. The slightly protruding jaw that made her perfect, as what woman could be perfect without some flaw? It was the gleaming white teeth, sensual mouth and button nose that had led to the Britney Spears comparisons. It was the complicated brows and bewildered forehead of the face's upper third that called to mind Barbara Stanwyck. I couldn't waste time admiring a forehead, however, even if I could get right into the scalp, see what at the roots made that black Italian hair so lustrous. No, I had to find my conduit.

I saw one kid tapping his foot at a six-tap per second rate. Upon entering his mouth I identified the distinct odour of a lunchtime Red Bull as the likely agitator. Another boy was giving a surreptitious Indian burn to his seating partner. This was not even oppositional defiance, just mundane cruelty. Then I saw her: dark bangs and glassy eyes, like some hybrid of Ally Sheedy in *The Breakfast Club* and the heftier of the two child perpetrators of the Slenderman slaying. If there wasn't something neurodivergent about her, if this was merely the face of contemporary grade seven girl malaise, then we were all doomed anyway.

"And your free writing assignment is due tomorrow," Adelle said as the bell rang, just as teachers were always saying things as the bell rang in the kinographic medium.

I followed the girl home, hoping she'd confirm my schema by killing a cat or two along the way, Randy Lenz-style, but she just whistled atonally while staring at the ground. In her shoddy bungalow I afforded her levels of privacy that wouldn't have even occurred to Big Rog. I was banking on a post-school nap, a favourite of the young/daily-growing but also of depressed persons. That was not to be. I waited for hours while she drew glyphs and symbols that I fancied indicative of something undiagnosed. She visited 4chan's /r9k board, also a good sign. Not a parent in sight, all this time. And nor yet had I caught her name, since she hadn't interacted with a single person; only interacted anonymously with her fellow robots on /r9k.

She consumed Diet Dr. Pepper after Diet Dr. Pepper. Knowing Dr. Pepper to be among the most caffeinated of pops, I feared this would not only prolong wakefulness but cause her sleep to be fitful. When she finally did nod off, I would have to work quick.

I pierced myelin sheaths and cruised Schwann cells as before. No angels or demons here, just a little army of Ally Sheedy/Slendy-murderesses doing awful things. In some corners of her mind she was castrating the Indian Rub guy with a rusty knife. In others she had the entire class bound and gagged while she did unsanitary things to their binders.

I turned into the wraith-equivalent of Marvel's The Flash, cleansed all those bad thoughts with light speed, light being the great disinfectant after all. And then I yelled it from the hills and in the halls, endlessly repeating the poem I'd been composing in my head since I'd seen Adelle in that slushy mall vestibule.

I learned of the big town news the next morning while peering over my father's shoulder at his desktop computer. His continued use of a desktop may offer insight into the man: many years previous I had offered him an old laptop of mine, citing convenience and superior processing power over his HP machine. He could never use a laptop, he'd scoffed, because he required a mouse. I'd explained how a mouse could be handily plugged into a USB port, causing him to wave his hand dismissively. Now he was at the point where he was dropping $5000 on a desktop because that's where the desktop market was at.

The man could navigate Internet Explorer though, give him that. On Facebook, his feed told of the great blows (rivalling those of Ermatinger's War of 1812) struck by John Doan, by Jill Gertz, by Amy Orlando, and by Patrick Gass, known and beloved to readers of this narrative as The Brapster.

A sampling of the headlines:

Publication: The New York Times
Header: Coordinated Graffiti at MOMA, Columbia, Guggenheim Blames Sacklers for Opioid Epidemic

Publication: Gothamist
Header: Just What in Fuck's Name is a Sault Saint Marie?
Sub-header: No, Seriously, We Had to Look It Up

Publication: New York Post
72-Point Frontpage Super-Header: Oxymorons!

The Sackler wing of Columbia University was open to students and faculty. This relative insecurity had allowed Jill Gertz to spray-paint "Sackler Opioids Are Killing Sault Ste. Marie" in two-foot letters right above the Sackler plaque.

The Museum of Modern Art, known affectionately to normies and art lovers alike as the *MOMA*, at 630,000 square feet, left a lot of ground for security to cover. This enabled John Doan to write "Sackler Scum Killed Sault Sainte Marie aka Pawateeg aka Ba-wa-teeg aka Sault Du Gaston aka Bawitigong aka Bow-e-ting aka Falls of St. Marie aka the Soo for $$" in blood-red letters large enough that pedestrians could not miss the increasingly-sloppy $s as they strolled along West 53rd Street that morning.

As a taser's electroreceptivity encroached upon Amy Orlando at the Guggenheim, she had the wherewithal to shorten her graffito to: "Sackler [skull/cross bones face] SS^," which might not have meant much if the hallowed Sackler halls of Columbia and the hallowed Sackler walls of MOMA had not already been graffiti'd with the full-throated indictment.

The *Sault Star* and other SSM-focussed Internet publications, provided with no press releases on the matter, initially published nothing regarding history's return to Baw-a-ting. They wouldn't have wanted to upload press releases about it anyway. In annual surveys, readers demanded more "good news." And so the *Sault Star* produced a yearly supplement featuring stories little more substantive than "Man Returns Quarter to Somebody" or "Art Gallery of Algoma Still Up and Running Thanks to Provincial Government Largesse." This was why, when the *VICE* film crew showed up to make their visceral *Steel Town Down* about the fentanyl epidemic, the general response from the town was: *We have an opiate epidemic?* The mayor was quoted as saying, "I had no reason to believe that it was any different here than it was anywhere else in Northern Ontario." People exchanged quizzical glances. And even then the documentary had been less than appointment television. If you had Nielsen numbers from SSM that Saturday night, it would have been beaten by *Singing Show* and *Better Times Rerun*. The lone *Soo Today* news article advancing the documentary began, "A documentary about Sault Ste. Marie, set to premiere during the final weekend of Bon Soo, promises to be quite the opposite of celebratory."

Since the anti-Sacklerian happenings were all over social media, however, the *Sault Star*'s Bob Stickman was eventually forced to summarize them with his usual mix of brevity and feeble-mindedness.

> *Publication:* The Sault Star
> *Headline:* Sault Vandals Bring Safe Injection Message to Big Apple
> *Sub-Header:* Graffiti Attack Raises Ire of City Famously Victimized by 9/11
>
> Four local youths, John Doan, Jill Gertz, Patrick Gass, and Amy Orlando are being held on charges of vandalism in Manhattan, New York, USA.

Doan, 21, Gertz, 19, Gass, 22, and Orlando, 24, spray-painted Soo-focussed messages aimed at Mortimer Sackler, thought to be the founder of Purdue Pharma, the company that manufactures OxyContin.

"Opioids are killing Sault Sainte Marie," read one message.

The landmarks targeted included the Guggenheim Art Museum, the University of Columbia, and the New York City Modern Art Museum, drawing the ire of New Yorkers, famously some of the most irksome people in the world.

David Perrault, a former Saultite working in Brooklyn as a sound designer, tweeted, "Sault Sainte Marie jerks ruin the Guggenheim. Sounds about right."

Many on social media linked the actions of the three local youths to the controversial Concerned Sault Sainte Marie Residents Against the Opioid Epidemic Who Are Nonetheless Advocating For Safe Injection Sites Cooperative.

"Somebody got in her head," said Amy's mother, Rachel Orlando, in an email interview. "That girl has never even been to Traverse City let alone New York. This isn't something she'd do on her own."

Constable Doug Bindi of the Sault Sainte Marie Fentanyl Crackdown Unit urged strong action against the CSSM-RAOEWNAFSISC in the wake of Monday's attack in New York.

"It's passing the buck. You don't blame Seagram's when some drunk driver veers off the road and his tires crush your daughter's skull. You blame and kill the driver. It's bad enough these safe injection cucks advocate for publicly-funded crimes right here in Sault Sainte Marie, but now they're out ruining our reputation in real cities."

The spray paint "attack on New York" was the focus of Adelle's Current Events class that afternoon. Why did they do it? How did they do it? What was fentanyl? What was New York? Where was New York? Had anyone's parents been to New York? No, no parents had been to New York? No? Had anyone seen a movie set in New York? No? Had anyone seen the television show *Friends?*

"I heard *Friends* was problematic," said one woke young woman.

"It might be. It might be problematic now," said Adelle, sounding tired, tired of the children, tired of keeping tabs on the new *problemas.*

"I heard from my dad that they want us to pay for junkies to shoot dope in the mall," said a strapping young man, no doubt bound for Progressive Conservative Party of Canada membership.

"I'm not sure if it would be in the mall. I think it would be at the hospital," said Adelle.

"I heard it's going to be where the Lazer Tag place is. They're taking away the Lazerium so the junkies have a place to shoot free government dope," said one apparent laser tag fan.

"Do you remember the discussion we had about fake news?" asked Adelle.

"Some people were sharing that *VICE* documentary from a few years ago and I watched it and it said there are like forty overdoses a day in Sault Sainte Marie but nobody talks about it," said a likely consumer of *VICE* content, in that he was only in grade seven, and yet wore those awful ear-expanding earrings that have mercifully gone out of style as all sane people knew they would.

"I guess it's how you define an overdose," said the class logician, "Like a lot of these people are just nodding off and then someone panics and sprays a bunch of Narcan all over the living room."

"The documentary said a lot of them want to die," spoke the *VICE* demographic-situated and lobe-stretched young man. "Maybe we should just let them die. And I'm not saying that to be a right-wing kleptocrat like Donald Trump because as you know I am not that. I just mean if they want to die then why are we shooting them full of Narcan and ruining their peaceful drug death? Not trying to be edgy, just telling it like it is."

"Thanks for that, Mitchell," said Adelle. "Except I'm sure these people have families who love them, so even if they want to die their mothers and fathers probably want them to live."

"That one guy in the documentary seemed like a real burden on his family," said one of the Sault's many generic Italian kids.

"Yeah, like their lives would be way better without that guy sponging off them," said a pudgier Italian.

As current events class concluded, the time for the main

event had come. English. Free-reading.

"Any volunteers to go first?" asked Adelle.

The neurodivergent girl raised her hand. This caused a stunned silence. I guess she was not known as the participatory type.

"Oh my god," said the most equine girl in the class, the quintessential "Oh my god" that has prevented the neurodivergent community from volunteering since time immemorial.

The Sheedy/Slendy-murderess then stood straight up, as I'd instructed her, cleared her throat, and read the following, which Capp has warned somewhat derisively against including in its entirety, but on which matter I have put my senior-editorial foot down:

I dreamt a screenplay that night
And knew the dreamt kino
Would keep me in the rooming house
Keep nutrients and pills in my stomach
Bring mirth and pathos to the world
And establish me as an important man of letters

But as I reached for my phone
As I opened notepad
The details scattered

Details of bathing suits
And hard-won seating arrangements
And the hilarity borne of the accusations
Despite the dark nature of the accusations

I didn't know how to format a screenplay
I didn't want to be one of these guys
30 years old
In the bread line

Talking about a screenplay
So I tried to forget the dream

"Second career is not a loan."
"It's money that the Ontario government is giving
away."
That's the language they use.
I'd been "negatively affected by the economy"
I was eligible

The Ontario Government asked only
That the field of study be "in-demand."
And there were already enough screenwriters.
So I would never be like Preston Sturges
The highest paid man in America

I had to learn tool and die
Architectural Technology
Medical Radiation Technology
Land Survey Technology
Men were needed to make cabinets

I chose radiation
But mere radiating wouldn't be enough
I had to take electives
To become well-rounded enough
To be trusted with the radiation

I chose Creative Writing
And on the first night
The teacher played a Dylan song
And told we cabinet makers, we operators of cranes
That a song could be a poem

And I thought of all the bad English teachers
I'd known in my life
And how in all their English classes

I'd sat beside the same girl

There was the great 300 pound man in grade ten
Who drank secret whiskey from a Pepsi bottle
And sent me to buy him cafeteria poutines
Later brought down by accusations

In grade eleven there'd been the woman with
hyperpigmentation
Opposite disease that Michael Jackson had
And she'd been invited on Oprah
But had declined
In 1995

And though she was a little white lady
With a perm
Turning black
One patch of skin at a time
In a racially homogenous steel town
And though we were predisposed to adolescent cruelty
As all the cruelly-adolescent must be
It was not hyperpigmentation we mocked her for

We mocked the way she said
"Drunken Tinker"
Over and over
"Drunken Tinker"
In her bid to wring some meaning
Out of *The Merchant of Venice*

Some said the girl resembled Britney Spears
Though she had dark skin
Like all the Italians in town
But to me she looked like Barbara Stanwyck
Leaning into Henry Fonda in *The Lady Eve*
I was forever that fool beer scion

I also sat beside her at swimming pools
At birthday parties
Where she'd worn bathing suits
That I can still remember
One in particular
In a sauna in the summer
That was almost see through

In Vitiligo's class
She would call me Bones
Because I was skinny
And I would call her Yokozuna
Because she was not

She'd gasp in mock outrage
And the girl in front of us would say,
"You two are terrible flirts."

I dreamt of winning victory
Over her Junior A boyfriend
To be like Kirk Douglas in *Spartacus*
But I was more like Kirk Douglas
In *The Strange Love of Martha Ivers*

After a presentation she gave
In OAC Writer's Craft
I raised my hand
And said,
"One question:
"Why are you so hot?"

Because then
We said "hot"
When we meant "beautiful."

She'd blushed and said,
"You're embarrassing me."

I think she'd loved it
And the crowd had loved it
As I was the comic M.C. of
That, the happiest class of all my days

I recall her saying to me
In the 300 pound man's class
"You really are cute . . . "
Like she'd thought it over
And then doubted
And then come to grudgingly accept

Or one time returning
From the neighbouring town's Pizza Hut
We saw the Nicolet Tavern
And she said in that innocent child-voice
She was so good at,
"It's my favourite tavern."

And then just last month
She'd been back in Sault Sainte Marie
With her dozen-odd kids
And I'd seen her at the Station Mall
Advertised locally as "the centre of it all."

And she'd seen me too
And she was hoping not to stop at all
But I saw her too noticeably
And we had to stop
Though she didn't even come to a complete stop
Kind of kept the stroller rolling
Along the brown mall tiles

Maybe it was concern over the purse snatchings
Or all the dragon-chasing accessories
Sold at the mall's many Dollar Stores
Or maybe it was just

One too many mornings
She'd woken to my wry Facebook messages
about the Vitiligo woman's transmutation

Or she'd woken to news links
Detailing the 300 pound man's
Trial, mistrial, second trial,
Conviction, heart attack, hospital stay
And eventual confinement to the penitentiary

All those little red flags
From some bygone comic M.C.
All those references to long-past OAC
While she was busy raising all those kids
Making all that cold press juice

And still strolling
Still rolling along brown tile
She said in the child-voice
She was so good at
"Hi Bones."

But no one wants to watch a movie
About a stroller that keeps rolling
Or the fairly quotidian indignity
Of losing out to (Lake) superior suitors
With a subplot full of dark accusations
About the 300 pound man
And the Vitiligo's progression

Besides, soon to be radiating
Commanding a type of
Radiation-related respect I suppose
I can still remember how she looked in all those
bathing suits

Poems of *Onyx*ian quality mustn't have been frequently shared during the free-reading period. Everyone sat stunned until the OMG horse-haired girl broke the silence by stage-whispering, "Oh my god, gay!" Recognizing an underdog he might champion, the *VICE* dogmatist tried to get a slow clap going, but everyone recognized his slow-clap as filmically-inspired artifice and so it ended only in his embarrassment.

Adelle, for her part, had hastily excused herself at the poem's conclusion, tissue in hand, perhaps moved by my tribute, perhaps a little creeped out by it, but more likely concerned that her armchair rational-materialism was no longer applicable given the current climate of occult happenings in Baw-a-ting.

The inexplicable assault on the Sackler legacy did not register with Maisie and her friends, whom I found assembled in Maisie's bedroom, all looking at their phones. Girls this age once looked at magazines. Who would ever look at *Seventeen* now besides Big Rog and his brethren?

On the topic of reprobation, Big Rog was on hand, putatively to fulfill his teen-abutting obligations to his conjoined Wraith of Mellissa Gladstone.

"How are things going, Big Rog?" I inquired.

"We're going by Roglissa now," said Rog.

As portmanteaux go, it was not a fine one, so I've elected to refer to them individually in this document, since it was pretty apparent to me who was saying what anyways.

"Everyone is sharing that *VICE* documentary again after the spray paintings," said the Rog faction of Roglissa, "So we went to the steel plant to see if it was bad as they made it out to be."

"And . . . "

"It's pretty bad. You can't really see how apocalyptic it is from the street. From the lake all you see are molten hot slag heaps and noxious piles of iron ore and stuff."

"Did you get those pills from your dad?" my sister asked Andie.

"No, it's so annoying."

Andie's father had been hospitalized yet again for "exhaustion" (Oxy overdose,) prompting her mother to throw away his stash "because they made him more tired when he was already exhausted enough."

"So . . . " said Jay, "Me and Darby have been talking. Like we're officially talking."

"He talks to everybody," hissed the Wraith of Mellissa, probably just counting the days until Darby OD'd so that she could join him instead of Big Rog in wraithly conjugation.

"And anyway I figured your dad might be exhausted again, so I asked if he can get us pills for Friday night. He swears they aren't the fentanyl ones. These are the ones straight from the hospital," said Jay.

"Aren't the ones from the hospital worse because they're like the patches that go on the old cancer woman who's dying anyway? Like might as well have the strong stuff since dying anyway?" asked Maisie.

"You're thinking fentanyl patches. These are just OxyContin pills. Like for knee sprains. Only like 40 milligrams. That's less than an Advil. An Advil is 200 milligrams. Some Advils are even 400 milligrams," said Jay.

"Maybe should just do some jello shooters. What if we get too exhausted to dance?" asked Andie.

The girls looked at her as if she'd suggested wearing a Minnie Mouse sweatshirt to the dance instead of the *de rigeur* tube top.

"Is it just me," asked the Wraith of Big Rog, "or is it a little nuts these kids are skipping weed entirely and starting with 40 milligram Os? When I was their age it was a big deal if you spread a little hash oil on a joint or something."

"It is not good," I said.

Jay received a text.

"Oh no. He's not going to be able to see me before the dance. Darby says his friend can drop them off tonight though. Can he come here?"

"I guess so. Maybe we just meet him out in the driveway," said Maisie.

"How's that look? Some hand-off in the driveway? We're not dope addicts," said Jay.

"Who is it?" asked Maisie.

"Allan something . . . " said Jay.

"Wait, that guy is friends with my brother kind of," said Maisie.

Texts were exchanged with Allan. While the girls fretted and nearly tore their hair out, sure that the Fentanyl Crackdown Unit would kick down the door and rape/kill them at any moment, Allan was getting a ride from some Aurora's line cook in exchange for a ten-dollar discount on a couple of 80s.

Allan knocked and gave the briefest of waves to my father, all "Regular here, sir, no need for a big to-do every time I pop by."

First he went to my brother's room, where David paid the full retail price for four 40mg Os, $160. I wasn't altogether sure where a fifteen-year-old gets that kind of disposable income. The first couple times maybe it's from some birthday card. Then things get cost-prohibitive. That's why, ideally, it's best not to start with 40mg Oxys.

Allan tapped a pustule or two for detectable ooze before knocking on Maisie's door. Here was inappropriate action worthy of the living Big Rog. My father would have been more vigilant about this type of impropriety during my rearing, so he must have been deeply distracted by his double-sided puzzle or possibly the grieving of my death.

Allan threw the pills on the bed. Jay handed over a wad of bills. Little girls always seem to have a lot of money, somehow. Allan didn't even offer to quarter the pills. It was a hell of a thing. Maybe Sacklerian overkill had decimated his prudence receptors. Maybe he dealt with thirteen-year-old junkies on the regular and couldn't tell the difference.

Regarding Jay's weight, Big Rog estimated a disturbingly specific 122 pounds. Andie, at nearly six feet tall and pushing two bills, was none of our concern. A 40mg Oxy on zero tolerance and the kidneys commensurate to a 100-pound frame like Maisie's, however, was a recipe for a second OD in the family, which really would have been going too far, of the Sacklers, of Acne Allan, and of even the town's boredom, which can't be discounted as a contributing factor in all this.

And sure, Bad Doug Bindi sat outside in his car, mentioning to his deputy how Acne Allan was making a lot of stops at this recent OD-associated dope house. But Bad Doug's sentiments were hardly even on my radar. And here Bad Doug will sort of make his way into the wings as the primary villain of this account.

What villainy can take centre stage is the scene found at the Opiate Awareness Flash Mob that afternoon, which had been moved up to take advantage of the natural publicity after the spray paint attacks.

Defined by Wikipedia as "a group of people who assemble suddenly in a public place, perform an unusual and seemingly pointless act for a brief time, then quickly disperse, often for the purposes of entertainment, satire, and artistic expression . . . " Sault Sainte Marie didn't quite grasp what a flash mob was meant to be, conceptually. Ours were practically biweekly by this point in history. The mobs rarely included more than the same dozen people, even after press releases were sent to the local press release mills to drum up interest, which advance interest-drawing obviously went against the whole principle in the first place. It was just the Sault's way of trying to put a hip spin on their little awareness gatherings, on their boom box music and uncoordinated grandma dancing.

Sensing a dearth of leadership from the nervous teenager who'd organized this Flash Mob Against Opiates, Margaret took charge. As someone who "stayed active," she called upon experience in another of her hobbies and assembled the ragtag mob into line dancing formation, though the song playing was not country/western but rather that old resistance standby, Twisted Sister's *We're Not Gonna Take It.*

My mom continually pulled down at her hastily-macraméd "We Stand Against Opiates" T-shirt. One woman, whom Bob Stickman would later style as *controversial,* wore a Titans of Thor leather jacket. A uniformed policewoman participated without the consent and indeed with the expressed non-consent of Bad Doug Bindi. This policewoman believed so strongly in *outreach* that she'd risk her badge and neigh well her life to reach out. The usual cadre of differently-abled people had been wheeled out from their group homes by the altruistic flash mobbers, so that they the differently-abled, but also they the flash mobbers, would have something to do.

This brings about two opportunities for analogy. The first, in keeping with the by now somewhat dreary theme of this work, is that the flash mob typifies how having "something to do" cannot be achieved through coercive means. You could not alert the good populace of Pawateeg to a flash mob and expect them to consider it "something to do." For something to be "something to do" it had to be something that people organically wanted to do. This was evidenced by the grimaces of extreme discomfort upon the visages of all mall patrons hurrying past the flash mob. No awareness was raised in them. They saw that something was being done and they smelled a rat. They knew it wasn't really something to do. They wouldn't make eye contact with Margaret though doing so was pleasant due to her eyes' greenish hue. The Opiate Awareness donations cup, like Big Daddy Cool during his run as WWF champion, would draw no dimes.

However, I will heed Capp's advice and look to the positive in this mob. All but Margaret and the teen dancer appeared deeply uncomfortable, yet they were making an effort to *do something*. Which is different than *having something to do*. They weren't sitting at home lamenting the lack of *something to do* while watching *Singing Competition* or *Better Times Rerun*. Nor were they snorting Sacklerian molecules. They were doing what they could. They were cognizant (barring, potentially, the cognitively-dissimilar figures wheeled from the group homes) of an issue, and though the issue has been painted somewhat broadly (opiates) and did not take into account the necessity of some opiates for surgery and legitimate pain and so forth, they stood, danced rather, against that threat, there in the irrelevance of the mall.

It's unfortunate that the peril of banking too heavily on one industry had never been made abundantly clear to the Margarets of the Sault, or else they might have organized mobs against the Sault's devolution into a sort of Russian *monotown*. They could have taken on the brain drain caused by the town putting all its chips on Algoma Steel in the very minutes preceding North American deindustrialization. They might have danced nervously against all that.

Here Capp would like to draw a corollary between our depressed state and that of Ah-an-ish-in-ab-ug back in the dream time: *To eat, drink and be merry while the store lasted was the highest good of existence. But when the game disappeared and days of searching failed to discover its haunt, then silently and despairingly would Ah-an-ish-in-ab-ug return to his lodge from the hunting, and sitting down by his slowly dying fire would give himself to despair.*

Bob Stickman appeared, wearing his eye patch and fedora, and given over to his own dogged and unspoken despair. He had to be there; he'd received the press release. Plus the flash mob was the day's lone news. Cameras from *LOCAL2* and *Soo Today* snapped eagerly, imbuing the flash mob with significance.

Unbeknownst to the disinterested scrum, that day's events would recall the days when local newsmen covered the violent strikes of 1903 or War of 1812 skirmishes. Today *LOCAL2* and *Soo Today* and Bob Stickman would be rewarded for their journalistic presence. Today that rarest of rarities would manifest in Bawitigong: actual news. For just as *We're Not Gonna Take It* was gearing up for its eighth repeat on the boom box, who should storm the food court but six frothing members of CSSMRAOEWNAFSIS.

"Shame, shame, shame!" chanted Deb Martin.

Margaret tried to turn the jukebox up, but this children's toy was already at max volume. Undeterred, Margaret danced with renewed purpose. I had to admire her. And not just for her aforementioned and ongoing Sophia Lorenian hotness, but for her obstinate demonstration that no negative chant could quell the positive spirit of awareness-raising.

"People are dying from not having a place to safely inject opiates!" Deb Martin shouted over Dee Snider's vocals.

"Isn't there already a clean needle exchange?" asked one of the wheelchair-bound persons. This startled a nearby Bob Stickman, who must have assumed this wheelchair-conveyed personage was too cognitively hard done by for speech, let alone rational arguments.

The flash mob participant in the Titans of Thor jacket cracked Deb Martin in the skull. It was a good knock. This flash mobber had thrown a few bombs in her time. One of Deb's cronies kicked over the toy jukebox, setting off a violent skipping fit. It had grown evident that neither party was going to take it. Mall security, both of them, wrangled the belligerents, leaving the handicapped bathroom free for Kapoorian injections inestimable. A few of the heftier women were contained by security using an ersatz, two-man "kettling" procedure. Unfortunately, this also led to the kettling of a wheelchair-bound person, not the one who'd made the rational point about the safe needle exchange, but the one who really did appear pretty far cognitively removed from the situation. This dear man, already stricken by cognitive disadvantage, was thrown from his chair to the slushy mall floor where he squirmed and moaned with the *LOCAL2* lenses affixed upon his suffering.

Sadly (and parenthetically) for Bad Doug Bindi, this was the afternoon that he drove halfway to North Bay to buy his bimonthly eight eight-balls of coke, so he wasn't around to make the bust, and other members of the Fentanyl Crackdown Unit were left to their own relatively liberal-minded approximations of busting Deb Martin's head and leading her off to the remand centre.

The teen organizer in tears and thus unavailable for comment, Bob Stickman approached Margaret for a quote on the melee.

"We just wanted to do something good for the town, to raise awareness of this important issue," she said through her tears, looking even more beautiful than usual.

But hey, let's keep on dancing, right? For tonight is the St. Mary's College Jessica Bindi Memorial Dance, ostensibly a fundraiser for the Sault Sainte Marie Fentanyl Crackdown Unit, but really just a good old-fashioned high school dance.

I was relieved to watch Maisie and her friends saw a single 40mg Oxy into thirds using a dull paring knife. Maisie took the median piece, Jay the largest, and Andie, reticent to begin with, was left with scrap powder and some blue anti-abuse coating.

David consumed his whole 40mg Oxy, not having bothered with inviting a friend over to share. While vibing on a *Final Fantasy XIV* soundtrack he halved a second 40mg Oxy to consume later in the evening.

The mall had smelled of low-grade cleaning product and Cinnabon, whereas the dance was redolent of Axe Body Spray, sugary perfume, and body odour. Tastes on the tongues of flash mob participants were cigarettes and halls cough drops. In the gym it was all cherry lip gloss and ice mint gum. While the majority of the flash mobbers were post-menopausal, here visible waves of testosterone and estrogen mixed in the air.

I was proud to observe David engaged with a girl who was cute, if only as a result of youth. His friends looked on from their hunched positions in moderate astonishment. I figured the gaming crowd rarely veered too far afield from the gym wall.

Acne Allan was also dancing with two of the better-looking girls at the dance. The gamers directed a few mean spirited jabs at Allan, who either couldn't hear the jabs or simply didn't care, engaged as he was in the only significant dance phenomenon of the past thirty years: grinding. The gamers had not yet put it together. They didn't yet understand the molecule that offered Acne Allan this confidence and joie-de-vivre. How could they know that $C_{17}H_{19}NO_3$ could bestow this gift?

I had ventured forth from the gamer wall to do some grinding in my time. As alcohol was the dirty and broad-acting lubricant in those days, naturally the night would peak early. I'd show up drunk as sin, grind like the devil himself for an hour, and then, as my blood-alcohol level ceased to rise and to produce an opiate-like effect as it does in those hard-wired for alcoholism, I'd fall prey to tiredness or anger or *douleur-de-vivre*. Still I'd enjoyed a fine hour or two. There'd been kisses with girls of minor beauty, if never with anyone that would have moved the Saliturian needle.

A grade eight dance was where I'd first encountered Adelle. We'd done the limbo. Simpler times, these. She'd been a dancer at Sensational Sherri Martel Dance Studio or whatever the hell it was called, and thus flexible. We'd danced closely, post-limbo. We'd been in each other's league then, unknown to each other in the dark, before I could say much of anything stupid with my too-deep voice. Years later, at a grade twelve dance, I'd seen her rejected by some titan of popularity rather than of Thor, and I'd been there to pick up the pieces, but she'd been dismissive, saying, "Not now, Tom," as our inequality was by then well-established and she'd been hearing my voice for far too long.

Maisie and her friends were not grinding. They were dancing amongst their own all-girl dance circle as girls are biologically mandated to do. The look of exuberation upon each and every one of their faces is beyond our meagre powers of description. The Wraith of Capp has ventured a description but I have chosen to leave it out due to an excess of what I consider purple language.

The Wraith of Mellissa Gladstone was right there trying to absorb all of that healing dance circle camaraderie denied to her in life. This provided Big Rog an excuse to cozy up to the all-girl dance circle. Big Rog was bobbing their collective wisps so as to dip into the vicinity of Jay or, less occasionally, Andie. When their conjoined wisps neared Maisie, I issued a stern wraith glance at Big Rog, causing Big Rog to reply with a little figurative head nod, *i.e.*, "Sure I might get an eyeful here and there, but tell me, has this become a crime? And please don't worry that I'll wraith-bob down in the direction of your sister's cleavage because that would sully our friendship, but realistically only because you are here observing and kind of killing my buzz."

Observance/vibe killing—Bad Doug Bindi was occupying these roles as official chaperone at this dance honoring his oh-so-dead daughter. Though it was a struggle given the strobe lights' fracturing of temporality, he stood by the DJ booth keenly looking for any suspicious powders snorted, dragon-chasing tinfoils set aflame, or surreptitious hypodermics. All while himself not even surreptitiously taking hard slams from his 1.25-litre flask that was so big as to barely even qualify as a flask anymore, and only somewhat surreptitiously going to the men's room every fifteen minutes for a key bump and every sixty minutes for a massive line off the back of a toilet seat.

So here, in short, was something for the young people in Baw-a-ting. They have manifested it for themselves. Of course that thing is little more than the promise of sex, still blessedly out of reach for most assembled. And soon even sex will get boring, and sooner still all the prettiest people will leave town, making dances like the Jessica Bindi Memorial the unchewable madeleines of bitter Proustian recall for Andie and Jay and all of we Sault-situated attendants of God.

Lacking anyone to grind, a dozen seniors and civically-inclined individuals were at that same hour attending a city council meeting. An aspirant filmmaker asked for many millions of dollars to finance production facilities that would bring "many millions more to the north." The filmmaker was then sussed out as being an agent of Big Telefilm and not even from the Sault. One councilman who'd been on the right side of a few thousand *Coconut Hero* dollars requested that security escort this man out.

A more trustworthy man in a soiled windbreaker asked that the putrid land by the sewage plant be rezoned for use as a driving range. With little about this proposal smelling off to council, they kicked it down the road for future council meetings. "Going forward, let's maybe look into doing something about doing something," said a forward-looking councillor.

I gauged it to be an average night. Under Capp's tutelage, I'd already wasted many hours reading council minutes and streaming their five hour meetings. Motions tended towards acts of civic derring-do no more controversial than "Be it hereby moved that the council is

100% behind our local special Olympian."

Quotidian financial hurdles did sometimes have an ersatz *Abbott and Costello* feel, like the selling of the former jail, at 36,000 square feet, for $199,000, half the cost of a 500-square-foot condo in Toronto. The stumbling point had been the missing remains of hanged convicts, a real recipe for unpleasant karma if not outright hauntings. Were hanged brigands often the stumbling block in civic real estate? I assumed not. Final resolution: kicked down the road.

Worst had been the motion carried in the wake of the *Steel Town Down* documentary. The whole evening should have been charged with fiery testimonials and emergency allocations for rehab beds and Narcan kits. Instead, and here we are quoting:

> Whereas the CTV W5 program "Steel Town Down" focused on the opioid crisis across Canada, and how it is affecting mid-sized cities like Sault Ste. Marie; and Whereas the program featured Sault Ste. Marie's Jamestown neighbourhood as one of the areas in Sault Ste. Marie where the use of opioids and other substances is prominent; and Whereas the Sault Ste. Marie Innovation Centre's GIS department has been presenting data to stakeholders in the community for a number of years on the lack of park services and outdoor recreation activities in the Jamestown area and throughout the downtown core; and Whereas the lack of activities in Sault Ste. Marie was cited as one of a wide number of factors that results in individuals turning to substance use, and ultimately substance abuse, in Sault Ste. Marie; and Whereas the provision of park services and outdoor recreational activities is an area of direct municipal responsibility and an area where the City can play a leading role in combating part of this issue; Therefore Be It Resolved that

Community Development and Enterprise Services staff, in consultation with the Innovation Centre's GIS department, be requested to bring forward to City Council forthwith a James Street and surrounding area revitalization plan, including, but not limited to: possible expansion of Anna Marinelli Park; conversion of unused green space in the area for recreational use; and an examination and assessment of James Street and a recommendation on how best to use James Street as a public space; and recommendations on the creation of a park or green space in the Downtown core.

Plan was to mow the lawn, essentially.

It was not the first time the council had opted for a quick fix at the town's enduring expense. Union-agitator John Ferris introduces his pamphlet, *Sault Ste. Marie in the Depression: The City and Its Citizens*: "The year was 1929; aspirin was the popular mood drug . . . Council instruct[ed] the City Engineer, and the Board of Works, to proceed with the construction of storm-sewers on John Street to help relieve the unemployment situation . . . Evidently, ignoring the needs of the times, the Sault was attempting to go it alone, in a band-aid manner, endeavouring to keep within its normal budget. It was clear [emphasis added] *that the gravity of the situation had made little impact.*"

The council appointed a City Unemployment Registrar, just as years later it would appoint a Sault Sainte Marie Minor Sex Abuse Unit, and a Fentanyl Crackdown Unit, and a Chief Operating Officer, just as it would launch its many inquiries into DeLuca and various spending snafus. The four hundred who'd applied to the registrar by the next day were denied liquor permits. None of them sought Suboxone; it wasn't around yet. Single men were denied meal tickets. Searchmont families subsisted on a potato diet.

L'il Arnie: "Beef for dinner tonight, ma?"
Ma, resigned as ever, "Potatoes, dear."
L'il Arnie: "Mashed? I do love 'em mashed."
Ma, lacking milk or cream, "Boiled Arnie. Boiled again."

Mass public meetings failed to fix the New York Stock Exchange, somehow. By 1933, Ferris writes, there was "fear for the coming winter. One of the political gimmicks that was fed the people was that 'prosperity is just around the corner.' Here it was three years, and it was still not around the corner." And here it was nearly a century hence, and those gathered at council were, in the words of the immortal Hulk Hogan, "Jabronie marks without a life that don't know it a work when you work a work and work yourself into a shoot."

In *The Great Depression in Northern Ontario*, Kathy McClelland-Wierbzbicki writes of a fear that has never quite left the Sault. As a woman named Mary Warmington faced a beggar at her door:

> I opened the door and there was a big Indian fellow there. He mumbled something to me and I didn't know what he was saying. I yelled "I'm going to call my father. He's in the other room." And the fellow said, "Don't get excited. I just want something to eat." But he was a real hobo, and I was really scared.

Foreigners were feared nearly as much as big Indian fellows. McClelland-Wierbzbicki quotes the city's relief officer as saying:

> Some of those who come here from foreign lands . . . are in the habit of sending all the money they can spare back to their old homes in Europe, where . . . a number of them have substantial bank accounts. It doesn't seem

right that they should be given relief here.

"Escapism . . . flourished in the north," McLelland-Wierbzbicki writes, "Probably the greatest form of escapism practised was that of daydreaming, a chance for the destitute to opt out of their troubles with . . . movie watching [and] radio listening . . . Liquor was a way out for some."

All of this is to say that agents of stupefaction were no new means of dealing with outside turmoil; nor were leanings, both vague and overt, towards ethnocentrism; nor was the council's fecklessness; nor yet a propensity for empty optimism among the populace of Pawateeg. This is evinced by the poem "Algoma Poetry" by Paul Hatton, quoted by McClelland-Wierbzbicki in her chapter on "Emotional Impacts":

> The thing to be done is to banish regrets,
> For they will not help us today;
> The present and future are what we must use,
> To drive this depression away.
> And so as we dwell on the outlook again,
> Contentment perhaps we shall find,
> Since most of our worries may turn out to be
> Naught else but the state of the mind.

Capp, always a suspiciously "merry" sort, proffers that we might close this depressive entry with a joke, the kind that keeps the old bags' eyes smiling in Bawitigong, from the *Sault Star* on January 21, 1931: "The bottom has dropped out of the egg market, what a mess!"

I woke the next morning to the sound of rolling thunder. And *when the thunder rolled ominously along the heavens it was because the Manido wished to warn his cowering children of the awfulness of his wrath and had released the birds who lived on human flesh.* Here it was not the Manido. Above Oak Park Crescent, well past Pino's House, well past the St. Mary's River and the diving birds called cormorants and the Cenotaph and the Cambrian Mall, the entire sky was filled with the largest and most malefic wraith I'd yet encountered. The Wraith of Mortimer Sackler had come to town.

I quivered under/through the covers, still withdrawing mind you, but possessed of the narratorial decency not to drone on about it, until my tossing and turning was interrupted by another presence in bed with me.

"The matutinal strolls at Bellevue have been quite solitary without you. Much to discuss and yet you spend your time chasing high school fancies and attending high school balls. Sad!" said the Wraith of Edward Henry Capp.

"Protocol at the rectory was it? Popping into any young man's bed with nothing by way of advance notice?"

"When we slept two-a-bed in those days, it was for

warmth."

"Same warmth Ken DeLuca was looking for I bet," I said.

"The perversions of a DeLuca scarcely existed before the twentieth century. I believe widespread DeLuca desires were perpetrated on mankind by the culture, by television, by glossed periodicals, all of which is to say—by Lucifer the devil."

"What about Albert Fish? He predated all that stuff and he was a real jerk."

"Happy to concede there were always a few fishy characters about."

"LOL," I said, encouraging Capp's rare attempt at humour.

"With much to celebrate, much to discuss, shall we to the park?"

We flew to Bellevue Park, with its goose dirt and its tetanus train, with its windswept expanses staring straight and majestically past the St. Mary's River, where once the Ojibwe could be found *[g]azing upon the tumbling waters, which are here forced through the narrow straits over a shallow bed of stone, their dashing spray shimmering in the sunlight, with here and there the ragged surface of a threatening rock exposed to view above the turmoil.*

"What now?" I asked. "We had our fifteen minutes. Tomorrow a prominent podcaster will say something problematic, a baker's intolerance will warrant public shaming, and Bow-e-ting's small marks upon the walls of Sackler will have been painted over, and meanwhile that all-encompassing hate-wraith you might notice above and around and even somehow throughout us looks like he means business."

"Not so. They'll come here, as good reporters must, as

Hemingway once did, when he remarked that 'the best rainbow trout fishing in the world is in the rapids of the Canadian Soo.' These brave scribes will tell the story of Sault Sainte Marie to the world. They will learn of Clergue, what started with . . . "

"Relying on golden era of journalism-style reportage? This is your plan? This is what I signed up for? Well, let me tell you something Mean Gene, a standard-issue mass slaughter gets two to four days in the news cycle. High scores of a dozen kills or fewer barely get a day. Clark's contextual import isn't going to register. Not on PBS. Not on the Clergue network. Not anywhere."

"They'll come and they'll know and things will be made right," shouted Capp.

"*VICE* came. They observed. It was nothing but a bad episode of *Intervention*. It changed nothing. I don't think we can record the type of history you recorded in 1903, bud."

As has been well noted, it's always trouble when a Canadian starts calling you *bud*.

"History is too fractured now," I continued. "Francis Fukuyama wrote that book *The End of History* after the Cold War, but then he looked like a real jerk himself because history started speeding up before the galleys were even sent out. History's speed increased so that the change of my month is the change of your bullshit lifetime, except it's all split off, different histories to different people: to my brother history is the history of the PSVR, Nintendo's early efforts at a virtual reality gaming system, and then his broader history is *Gaming Historian* videos about the launch of the 3DO. I have sat and watched him throughout the cruel hours of my afterlife and my withdrawal. His 3DO launch is what the fall of the Roman Empire was to you.

139

This is the new history. Nothing defines an era. OxyContin doesn't define us any more than the Internet does. And then the Internet is only everything, branching out into every tributary of German piss bukkake to the r/funny sub-reddit where humour goes to die to . . . "

"Young man you are rambling. The reporters will come. The good newsmen always must. Why, just as Hemingway said of the rainbow trout. . . "

"Enough with Hemingway's trout. The guy catches one trout and I'll be hearing about it for eternity. You want someone to take notice? I've got *Sault Star*-tier news for you. Someone did. And it's the evil and avenging Wraith of Mortimer Sackler," I said, pointing once more to the malefic Sackler clouds above us.

"Wholly aware of Sackler's bootless presence," remarked Capp, "Best left ignored, really. Certain personages, and here I think of Sir James Dunn, who have practised puffery throughout their living existence, Thomas, they remain puffed up in death. They go about, larger than us for certain, but nothing more than a lot of heated air. Outside of minor electromagnetic interferences, they remain harmless. Go to hell, Sackler, murderer! How's that? Not a thing he can do. He can kill millions for profit. He can kill millions to be among the first inductees to the Medical Advertising Hall of Fame. He can do nothing here in Baw-a-ting."

"Eat a dick, Sackler!" I cried.

A mighty wind descended upon the St. Mary's River. The water lapped up and over the banks, in and around on itself, forming a tiny typhoon. The typhoon was shaped like three-quarters of an egg, calling completely to mind the copyrighted symbol for Purdue Pharma that even in death I do not have permission to reproduce in this book.

I abandoned the matutinal stroll to follow Morty Sackler. He wasn't hard to keep tabs on. Tendrils of Sacklerian rot had spread throughout the town. He could be found in the Cambrian Mall food court, not even really a food court anymore, just a Subway with too many tables around it. He was on Pim Street and McDonald Avenue waiting at the red lights. He was with the welding apprentices at Sault College. He was up at Searchmont, in the chalet, with the alcoholics. He was on Tancred, and Bruce, and Denis, and Elgin and March Street. He was primarily, along with so many of the pills he'd foisted into the marketplace, in Jamestown.

Curiously, he was heavily concentrated in the top soil surrounding the St. Mary's River. Much as he'd convinced 1960s housewives they needed Valium, his flim-flam now ran through the one-track minds of worms and insects and snakes, convincing them that their current situation was as untenable as the housewives' had been, and while valium wasn't manufactured in worm-sized doses, the worms could squirm and writhe in such a way as to weaken the firmament, and in this rebellion against the natural order they might find peace. Like Kerouac's *Doctor Sax* before him, Sackler knew his way around the earth and soil: *He was no city shroud.*

Next he appeared at the Sault Sainte Marie Anti-Erosion Task Force offices, where good Graeme Abbot had made all sorts of self-oaths to snort no more than one 40mg Oxy per night shift if he even snorted any 40mg Oxys at all. Sackler got in his brain and convinced him otherwise, placing G.G. Abbot on the nod during Dr. Sacks' opening salvo of worm-based erosion.

"Why do you do it?" I asked the Wraith of Mortimer Sackler.

"I like to help people," he said earnestly.

Listen, Mortimer Sackler didn't build an empire of pain one junkie at a time. He built it with a massive sales force of strippers, real estate hustlers, and two-bit cons. His plan for eroding Bawitigong out of existence would involve a lot more than a few snakes and the opiated ambivalence of good Graeme Abbot. We should have known better than to attack such a shrewd old devil. He was a captain of industry; we were little more than two pseudo-intellectual dandies.

The Wraith of Capp and I helplessly observed his multifaceted plan unfold over the weeks to follow. His initial manoeuvres seemed insignificant, almost petty, wherein Dr. Sacks infected the dreams of the most desperate addicts, planting visions of a great cache of OxyContin bottles buried along the shore of the St. Mary's River. This had some minor efficacy, drawing out a few junkies with shovels, but since the shoreline extended several kilometres, these junkies were barely more useful to Sackler than his worms.

Sackler then convinced a few of the town's neurodivergents to plant Oxy bottles along the shore. The occasional find kept the diggers motivated for a while, but after digging all day for Oxy and finding none, one's approach to life is drawn into question such that visiting the nearest Jamestown dope house for some fentanyl once again feels like the smart play.

Capp and I tried to form a resistance, infiltrating others' dreams, suggesting that earth-digging for OxyContin was plain silly. We might even have had Dr. Sacks in check until the accident occurred, just outside Echo Bay, well within the confines of the windbreak.

A long-haul trucker was listening to a *Coast to Coast AM* episode on the opiate epidemic, ironically enough, occasionally drifting into a hypnagogic state, allowing Dr. Sacks to convince him that just one more 80mg Oxy, if taken judiciously, *ergo* orally, would have more of a stimulating effect upon his sensorium than a sedative one.

Dr. Sacks, possessing aforementioned electromagnetic powers, being on a first-name basis with the clouds it often seemed, then manifested some freezing rain. As the wheels veered on slick Highway 17, as the truck jackknifed, the latest Pharma shipment from Toronto exploded along with the majority of the truck's trailer. Echo Bay residents ignored the burning driver's cries of unceasing agony to fill their pockets with those pills least aflame. By the time the mayor of Echo Bay called the OPP, the driver had been long since immolated at the altar of Sacklerian enthusiasm.

Bad Doug Bindi got word of the accident and called in a hazmat team to scorch any remaining Oxys in chemical baths, as though just touching an opiate might turn a man into Big Rog. Yet the wheels were on fire and in motion. Dr. Sacks knew well that nearly every Oxy retailer (pharmacy) in North America worked on a just-in-time delivery system. Without this shipment the town would be bone dry in a week. Sure, the town's DOC was fentanyl by then, but good old Oxy was still holding down the fort among legitimate pain sufferers, nascent addicts, the rich, *etc.*

These Oxy users soon stormed the Shoppers Drug Mart, all in vain, until inevitably they turned to fentanyl, placing a concomitant demand on the fentanyl economy's own just-in-time delivery model. The unprecedented Sacklerian hysteria to follow made the withdrawing townsfolk susceptible to Dr. Sacksian dreams of diamonds in the dark soil, all to be found by the river that had sustained us for centuries.

As the dreams spread, so did talk of the dreams. It came up at the Tim Hortons. "You dream about all them pills too, eh?" It manifested at the GoodLife sauna: "Fuck if I didn't have the same dream, eh." No longer did digging all day seem like such a waste of time. As a single pill came to rival the cost of an economy car, the affluent found it prudent to invest in the hiring of a backhoe or two.

Even Graeme Abbott couldn't ignore all this, but the Anti-Erosion Unit was more or less keeping mum, due to all the violent menace in the air. An AEU press release to *Soo Today* and *LOCAL2* did assert that digging up the entire shore of the St. Mary's River with backhoes couldn't possibly be option A, in terms of anti-erosive end goals.

Adelle Salituri's classes continued as scheduled for the first weeks of the crisis. The erosion/shortage issues were a frequent topic of Current Events class.

"My dad says it's a conspiracy by Shoppers to raise the prices," said an Italian.

"*VICE* should be here making a documentary about the erosion and the Oxy shortage," said the ear-expanded kid. He'd taken out the ear expanders. Even he, at eleven, had gotten wise to the trend's nadir, but not before his young lobes had been distended in the fashion of a Salvador Dalí clock, for life, we hope, if there is any preventative justice left in this cruel world.

"I don't know, *VICE* was just here so they probably don't ever want to come back," said a young Scotsman, these not being quite so rare, given that *Scotsmen, travelling from the Hudson's Bay posts in the North back to civilization through the forests and over the rivers, tarried for a time and finally settled Sault Sainte Marie, stamping the impress of their nationality upon the settlement.*

"Yeah, it's like when *The Amazing Race* did an episode here," said an unwitting descendant of Chief Shin-Ga-Ba-

Wos-Sin, "And I thought, hey maybe they'll make TV shows here all the time, but after that it was just those Canadian shows that aren't really real shows, you know?"

"I do know," shouted an unwitting descendant of Ermatinger, "It's like when you're watching a hockey game on the CBC and they're like, 'Hey watch *Murdock Mansion* or *Debra Wong Mysteries* or whatever trash they're trying to pass off as real TV, when it's like yeah, I could just change the channel and watch real American TV."

"You know our tax dollars pay for all that fake Canadian TV right?" said, I suppose, the class spending reform wonk. "So it's like money out of your pocket is paying for those *Murdoch Mysteries* that no one is even watching so then even more money out of your pocket is paying for advertising for *Murdoch Mysteries* and why? Why? The CRTC was built to . . . "

"I think we're veering a little off topic," said Adelle.

"My mom went crazy and started digging up the ground," said a more doleful Italian.

Adelle too looked doleful as the emotional buttress she'd built around Sault Sainte Marie boredom and low-level suffering was eroding away like her native soil itself.

"Is it possible to view the town's erosion by Oxy freaks like Mario's mom as a metaphor for how time-released OxyContin kind of ruined the town? 'Cause even a few years ago, you know, back in the day, 2014-ish, in grade one, I don't remember it being this bad. Like I could go to the washroom at the library and there wouldn't be a junkie shooting dope there. Was it this bad when you were young, Ms. Salituri," asked an individual nostalgic for days gone by.

"No, it was quite nice actually," she said wearily.

Later that day, as Adelle reposed for a nap, I flew around

Adelle's healthy brain at light speed to unfurl a turn-o'-the-millennium Soo-schema relative to me. Imagery of a lakefront cottage. The temperate breeze off Lake Superior in the 30°C afternoon had strong roots in her sense memory. At this cottage on this afternoon we'd been in the sauna and she'd worn the borderline see-through bathing suit described so elegantly in my *Onyx*-tier poem. Obviously the see-through bathing suit held no emotional resonance for Adelle, so I neglected her recollections of my leering in favour of those from the Dodge Caravan ride home—

I'd been on the verge of dating a plain-looking girl, the diametric opposite of my desired Saliturian aesthetic. I was sitting in the middle seat between this wall-floral young woman and glowing Adelle, *sitting bitch*, as we called it then, and of course I couldn't resist joking with Adelle and Adelle couldn't resist the attention until the plain and pale and not even Italian girl whose brother went on to moderate NHL goaltending success said to us, when asked why she was being so quiet, "Well, maybe if you two would stop flirting."

This was the memory manifested of better days in Sault Sainte Marie as Adelle flitted between sleep and dreams. I'd fraudulently stamped my Accutanean teenage face on her memory: behaviour no more ethical than Dr. Sacks' erosive mind manipulations. And why? All for the same type of greed. Sackler wanted money at first, and then he had all the money, so he wanted power, and then he became a meme representing evil, so he wanted to clear his evil name. Once the Sacklers had tasted of death, mere wealth would never suffice. *The Indians hold to the belief that he who has once tasted human flesh becomes an evil spirit embodied in fleshly form, in their own language, becomes a "windigo," and can never be satisfied with other food.* With Adelle, I had tasted not of death but of life.

What was I doing it for? Why, when alive, was I not satisfied with other food, namely six-packs and games of bocce and backyard barbecues in verdant Pawateeg? It is possible, well-nigh probable, offers Cap, that I am just some kind of plaintive and past-fixated bloviator and that none of this is relevant to the history of Bawitigong whatsoever. And that while *one may be disposed to overlook the vagaries of poetic natures, it can hardly be admitted that such writings are pardonable, for misrepresentation in popular form is the most successful way of stirring up and keeping alive bitternesses which would otherwise die away.*

A few days later, as aggression against both soil and man escalated, I observed my sister and her friends discussing the matter in her FB group chat:

Maisie Kay: Guys my dad said the whole city is falling into the river. ☹

Jay Allysa: I haven't heard from Darby in three days I'm a little worried he might have fallen into the river too. ☹

Sam Caputo: He probably overdosed on time-released 80mg OxyContin pills you herpes slut. ☺

[Jay Alyssa REMOVED Sam Caputo FROM THE GROUP CHAT]

Jay Alyssa: Why did we let her back in again?

Maisie Kay: Do you think we'll have to move if the whole town sinks into the river?

Andie: It'd be cool if we got to move to Toronto or Vancouver.

Jay: Yeah, I doubt it. We'd probably just have to move to Echo Bay or Bruce Mines.

Maisie Kay: I'm so bored since we're not allowed to go to school or the mall because of the riots and the bodies strung up and the gunfire.

Andie Tomlinson: I still have my leftover Oxy from the dance. Thinking of doing it. SoOOOOO bored.

Jay: Same! But I heard they're going for like $1000 a pill so thinking maybe I could sell it.

Andie: Just looked in my dresser and mine's gone. My dad must have taken it. He's been acting less exhausted lately but he has a really bad cold and diarrhea and so our whole house is getting really gross and I can't even go outside because of bodies strung up my mom says.

Maisie: That's weird because my brother also has a really bad cold and diarrhea.

As a result of this "cold" and this diarrhea my father, finding his household increasingly malodorous on both an olfactory and psychic level, had doubled down on his snow-blowing regimen. All while my mother offered Imodium and Pepto Bismol and made obvious enabler/denial comments about "a nasty bug going around," even though the only things going around were massive bouts of opiate withdrawals.

And who could be withdrawing harder during this time than poor Acne Allan, who'd been up to a nearly inhuman 1300mg of Oxy a day. I followed him to the fat kid's house one afternoon.

"What say I buy back a few of those 40s I sold you just the other day," Allan asked Raphael, "Happy to pay a 10% premium. 15% even."

Raph laughed in sheer incomprehension.

"Allan, you pizza-faced rat boy, I'd been happy to see you, really had been, had sold my boat in anticipation actually. And now you come to me with this."

Raphael placed his literal fingers around Acne Allan's withdrawing neck and literally wrung it, right in front of the fat kid, who, God bless him, was still content with his Coca-Cola Classic. It was hard to blame Raphael, as sea crafts had by then become less a hobby and more a means of survival.

A flash mob against erosion was organized but failed to pick up much steam. A second flash mob description, Capp warns, may enter the realms of non-fictional excess.

Instead, Capp insists, we really should breathe non-fictional life into the murdering of Bad Doug Bindi. His slayers were the gang of seemingly-troglodytic highwaymen that had taken to raping and pillaging along Highway 17S, right where Trunk Road met the highway, meaning they weren't even highwaymen so much as "edge of town men," but no less murderous, mark us well. Anyway, since we were not there to witness Bad Doug Bindi's murdering at the hands of the highwaymen, there's little left to be said but RIP Bad Doug Bindi. ☹

And here, Capp suggests that I might apologize to the reader, as previous descriptions of Bad Doug Bindi stalking Acne Allan and eavesdropping on my 13yo sister were quite the (and forgive the phallocentric turn of phrase) *cock tease*, as they seemed to predict a tragic climax involving such beloved characters in this narrative. I argue that no apology is necessary, as this is a factual document meant to stand alongside books like *Dreamland: The True Tale of America's*

Opiate Epidemic, or *Dopesick,* or *The Story of Baw-a-ting: Being the Annals of Sault Sainte Marie.* While reporting dispassionately upon Bad Doug's East Side Mario's recognizances, I could not have foreseen that the Wraith of Mortimer Sackler would erode the town away and some stinkin' highwaymen would deprive readers of the pay-off they must have been both dreading and emotionally invested in.

Erosion continued. The AETF would show up with their bullhorns, but half the town was there angrily digging and back-hoeing and the AETF weren't even armed. The Fentanyl Crackdown Squad, grieving the murdered Bad Doug B, had marshalled the City Police and Fire Services for crowd control purposes. Their preferred means of crowd control was to fire assault rifles from the roof of the Korah Public Library while painting their faces with the blood of their enemies and shouting semi-pagan allegiances to the legacy of the late, great, Bad Doug Bindi.

All this blood running on the streets led to a brief and ultimately embarrassing declaration of martial law by, in Capp's words, "the notably feckless Prime Minister of the period." The declaration was not the first time the military had fecklessly occupied Baw-a-ting. In 1903 riots occurred as a result of Clergue's poor management of his enterprises. He could not meet his $170,000 payroll, causing 7,000 workers to smash windows and call for Clergue's head on a platter, perhaps next to some boiled ham and Soo Rapids whitefish. By the time the military arrived the men had grown weary of rioting, and the military simply ran up a huge tab at the Iroquois Hotel, which hotel really was nicer than any building that has stood since in Pawateeg.

Because of the Prime Minister's father's hotly contested history around martial law declarations, and because the soldiers arrived just as the next shipment of OxyContin made it to the Shoppers, and just as the U.S. Army Corps of Engineers arrived to get the shoreline situation under control, there was a lot of pushback from that most vocal voting block of Twitter users who believed that drug-fiending rioters and murderous highwaymen should not be militaristically oppressed. Sensitive to such pushback, the "feckless" P.M. called the martial law off after twenty-four hours. When military intervention would become truly necessary mere weeks later, this Prime Minister of the period would be scared to pull the trigger.

The OxyContin 80mg pills returned to the Shoppers. "These things are going like hot cakes," spoke the bald pharmacist, wearing his gravedigger's grin. The fentanyl time-released patches returned to the Rexall. Some of the junkies, known to the Rexall bean-counters as "customers," hadn't the time to properly boil the fentanyl out of their patches at home, so they sunk to a new low, placing the patches directly onto their foreheads upon receipt, in plain view of the Rexall pharmacist and his many interns. This Pakistani pharmacist wore no gravedigger's grin. He said to the sufferers, who all looked like idiots with their patches on their heads, "Please only use as directed." And then he said to an intern, "I entered the field . . . to . . . help people." And then he looked around. And then he shook his head.

The Suboxone and methadone returned to those independent pharmacies forced to cater to their dependents. These maintenance users appeared predominantly as upstanding citizens, yet the Shoppers did not want them lined up at 8am right when some minimum-wage earning Shoppers key holder unshuttered the doors. Because then some grandma is there for toilet paper or a granddaughter's tampons and sees the line of Suboxone/methadone-dependents, asks them if it's a line to get in the store like maybe it's Black Friday and she forgot, so one of them just says wearily, "I'm here for my drink," and the grandma doesn't really understand, but knows it has something to do with drugs, immeasurably darkening her day such that she's buying her granddaughter's tampons at Walmart from then on.

Anyway, as Capp is again over my shoulder and clicking his wraith tongue and generally "tut-tutting" regarding my tendency towards digression: all this is to say that the pharmaceuticals foisted forth by John Kapoor and Big Art Sackler and Morty Sackler (who has an English climbing rose named after him, incidentally) were back in a big way, and due to the withdrawals so many had been suffering, the molecule felt finer than e'er it had before.

The good U.S. Army Corps of Engineers set to work with their American know-how. They would strengthen the vegetated buffers that had been eroded by backhoes, install waterbars, dig drains, and erect silt fences. When an occasional Clergue-house dweller or Clergie tried to kick down a silt fence, the Corps would liaise with the AFCU vis-à-vis the application of deadly force.

When the silt fences and waterbars proved unsatisfactory, an ArmorMax anchor-reinforced vegetation system was put in place to provide long-term protection. As an abundance of caution, a stone revenant was ordered from whoever ships and manufactures 50-tonne stone revenants.

We considered breathing a sigh of relief. The town had suffered and would maybe rise up again. We'd survived the flood of 1916. We'd sent 3,000 men to fight in the Great War. We'd each of us suffered some sort of Saliturian rejection along the way. What was a little high-school heartbreak? What was a little erosion? What was a heinous uptick in molecule dependence?

As it always did, life continued its vague decline in Baw-a-ting. The OxyContin flowed through the community bloodstream. Having learned of the shortage days previous, the Xalisco boys showed up with their best black tar heroin. Here readers are referred again to Sam Quinones' excellent *Dreamland: The True Tale of America's Opiate Epidemic* for a more detailed description of Xalisco Boy ways and means. Anyway, deadly ODs by the score. Narcan about as frequently employed as suntan lotion at the Sandals resorts we Saultites depended on so broadly. Bad Doug Bindi was buried as inland as possible. I tried in vain to adopt an interest in Toronto Maple Leafs hockey for a while. The bingo hall and the library were reopened, even if there was still some brain matter and blood yet to be sprayed from the brown tiles outside of the Shoppers in the Cambrian Mall. Things (structures, playsets, family pets) kept falling into the river. Those living closest to the river inched a little further away each week, to a relative's, or to a motel.

I saw the sun setting on Sault Sainte Marie. I flew around for a bit, ruminating on the only home I'd ever known, covering a lot of ground.

At the Station Mall, the two security guards were no match for the *Walking Dead*-tier assemblages of freshly-opiated mall visitors. A bedraggled individual at the cell phone kiosk was telling his woeful story of his many destroyed SIM cards as he pawed kiosk phones and dickied with SIM-release mechanisms. A white man with dreadlocks stood rapping in the Arabica "bistro." Either the baristas were friends with this man or just abnormally tolerant of his TTC-quality rapping. At the Coles, a man swayed hazily in the research section, ostensibly researching standard preparations for the LSAT, but really just affecting the attitudes of the insane person. Here was the amphetaminic brethren of the dope fiend. He had foregone the poppy, or maybe indulged in the methamphetaminic arts, only to offset the stupefying effects of the poppy, and now he was inclined towards a purpose: to prepare for the Law School Admissions Test, to become adept in a field. He could have consulted the Internet on his phone, for certain, but we'd wager his in-Coles research had something to do with his own lost or confiscated SIM card and the stringency of the various gatekeepers he could not bypass or otherwise outsmart in order to access Tim Hortons' WiFi or whatever.

I found the ear expander/lobe-ruined kid posting something on Reddit's r/todayilearned board that I couldn't bring myself to read. He was looking awfully self-assured about it too.

Adelle and the accountant were arguing about the rapid amortization of their rental properties now that the town was being washed off to sea. Adelle wore the good old maroon St. Mary's Knights sweatshirt, and a ceiling-abutting wraith could still make out the shape of her excellent figure. This accountant had it all, but was concerned only with equity for some reason. But then who am I to judge? I cared for synthetic Sacklerian joys when I could have directed all my life's energies towards that which existed within that cotton sweater.

I found Big Rog and Mellissa at the Country Style where the NA wraiths hung out when the NA meetings weren't in session. Mellissa was accusing Big Rog of spending altogether too much of his afterlife in girls' change rooms and La Senzas and other places that struck the Wraith of Mellissa as not just creepy but also a huge snooze since how many teenage change rooms could she be expected to view throughout her eternity of conjugal attachment to Big Rog?

Also in the Country Style was the Wraith of Rex, whom readers may (or as likely, may not) remember as my father's employee who crushed his own leg for OxyContin. The Wraith of Rex was once more discoursing on his contempt for the A&E television program *Intervention,* saying, or screaming more like, "And whenever they could get one of them tarts whoring herself out and shimmying into little short shorts don't think them cameramen weren't instructed to get a nice tight shot of those butts and those legs and don't think those creep producers didn't just love it when the meth-head girls were kinda sexually flirting with their own fathers they're so strung out and depraved and don't think it ever crossed those producers' minds that airing that footage might have embarrassed them dads because once they signed that waiver that was that."

Deb Martin had decided to take matters into her own hands, setting up a three-man tent with a crudely Crayola'd piece of cardboard reading "Deb Martin's Safe Injection Site" at Bellevue Park. She neglected the giant acronym after a falling-out with the other board members regarding buy-in from community stakeholders. Bob Stickman wasn't there to report on the site opening because either Deb hadn't provided a press release or hopefully Bob Stickman had been killed in the riots.

The Brapster was being extradited back across the International Bridge, in handcuffs, in the backseat of some special-purpose extradition van.

The Butter Chicken Factory was empty as always. No one was boxing the BoxClub boxing arcade game. The *Halloween Store!* remained boarded up, the *Halloween Store!* sign still mocking us all, particularly those who might have a hankering for a spooky candelabra in the dawning days of spring.

At the fat kid's house, Raph was happily handing over wads of currency to Acne Allan in exchange for the Xalisco Boys' best black tar heroin. The recent strangling episode was water under the bridge, just as water from the St. Mary's River was soon to be water atop the very land mass sustaining us all.

Allan returned to his home, handed his father several bags of black tar heroin, and not yet having invested in a safe, simply stuck his duffel bag full of money at the back of his closet. He continued on his rounds, handing out black tar heroin samples to those customers still claiming to prefer OxyContin.

"Of all the great reasons to do heroin, the best one is that it's never going to be cheaper than it is right now!" he'd tell customers. "Got plenty of Oxy, sure, but why not give this gooey substance the old college try. Looks menacing, a little like the comic book antihero, Venom, sure, but no need to inject it, I assure you, though I do notice Deb

Martin with her nursing experience will facilitate that for you in some shoddy Bellevue Park tent. So yeah, just smoke away, same dragon chasing process you already know and love."

That's how my brother David got his first few bags of black tar heroin. That's how he was cooking heroin with a barbecue lighter on a sheet of tinfoil with one shaky hand and trying like heck to suck it all up through a tiny straw with the other. Here's how he was evoking an unbecoming mix of concern and outright jealousy from my own observing and withdrawing wraith consciousness. Here's how he was stinking up the entire second floor. Here's how he was over that cold, as my mom observed. Over that nasty bug that was going around.

Good Darby re-emerged—had not fallen into the river after all. He'd just been holing up in a Clergue House with some strong beer and some Clergies, watching his native soil get hacked up.

I observed this FB conversation:

Maisie: Want to go to East Side Mario's Tonight?

Jay: I think it's more of an Oxy night. I haven't had a nice nod-off in a while.

Andie: Yayyyy! Let's nod off guys! Sleepover.

I caught Capp at the library archives in the middle of his luncheon: turtle soup, baked Soo rapids whitefish, boiled ham in a champagne sauce, baked stuff heart with chow chow relish, huckleberry pie, and not a bite of it was anything more than a wraith wisp.

I thought the archivist might be archiving stories of the erosion and the Martial Law declaration, but he was just playing Farmville on his Facebook like he always was.

"You certainly brought history back to Bawitigong," I admonished Capp.

"Indeed. Does the stand being made by the good Army Corps of Engineers not call to mind the stand made by Ermatinger in the War of 1812?"

"Except the Army Corps of Engineers is from the U.S. side," I said.

"We struck the first blow, knowing too well a retaliatory one would come hence. We in Baw-a-ting have only just begun to fight. You'll note that Sackler has not yet responded to my challenge of a wraith duel."

"Thing is all that spray paint was gone like twenty hours later. So I feel the gloomy Wraith of Dr. Sacks has perhaps struck the decisive and final blow and can't even be bothered to respond to your challenge since it would be pretend wisp guns in the duel anyway."

So there sat Capp and myself, haunting the Korah Library while we could before its inevitable kerplunking into the St. Mary's River, still hoping the archivist would start scanning relevant documents or at least putting them in waterproof boxes, when the Wraith of Bad Doug Bindi popped his head in the door.

And when we say *head*, really the Wraith of BDB bore no resemblance to a human, as Capp and Big Rog and Rex all did, simply as a creature comfort rather than any kind of wraithropomorphic necessity. BDB instead chose to manifest as something akin to a 40' by 40' cauldron of righteous anger, the anger itself having a reddish hue evocative of lava or whatever contents of a witch's cauldron create that hue in cartoons.

"Deloooooooooooooooooooooooooooooooooooooocaaaaa aaa . . . " howled the Wraith of Bad Doug in his immortal hell howl.

"Seems another wayfarer wishes to learn of the history of Baw-a-ting!" said indefatigable Capp.

The archivist then experienced a chill, and put on his archivist's cardigan. I had been able to affect no chill in this 73-year-old man despite my immense disdain for him and my frequent attempts to "rattle" him, to use a favoured bit of Sault Sainte Marie parlance.

"DeLuca documents are suspiciously absent from this so-called institution of learning," said Capp. "Scant few do exist for those with the time to dedicate. However, before we can come to any understanding of the heinous crimes of DeLuca, we must commence with the Pot-ta-wat-tam-ie or *those who kept the fire.*"

"Really I think we can skip the Pot-ta-wat . . . " I began.

The Wraith of BDB then overtook both Capp and myself, filling our figurative wraith heads with visions of his own existential darkness.

The gist was: Bad DB's own daughter had been a victim, not of DeLuca, but of some spiritual descendant thereof, and *ergo* had become OxyContin dependent herself, and then exited the mortal coil by her own hand, leading Bad Doug to form the Sault Sainte Marie Minor Sex Abuse Unit in the interest of bloody recompense. This can all be chalked up to DeLucaean transference. The culture of sex abuse perpetrated by DeLuca had lingered and led abstractly to Bad Doug's daughter's own suffering, felt Bad Doug B, though he might not have been able to express it in those words, his preferred means of expression being the cracking of a kneecap here and there.

Readers craving further DeLucaean context are referred to the Ontario Attorney General's *Robins Report* of 2000, from which we've excerpted this particularly-heinous summary:

> The abuse reported by DeLuca's survivors included kissing students; inserting his tongue into students' mouths; rubbing his body against the students; touching or rubbing students' breasts; having a student hold his penis while class was in session; lying on top of students and rubbing his body against theirs; touching students' genitals; rubbing his pelvis against students; biting a student's chest and vagina through her clothes; and intercourse (with one student). The adult survivor disclosed that DeLuca grabbed her and, with his knees splayed, pulled her tight into his body while he made rutting noises with his pelvis against her private parts.

Survivors also maintained the following acts of harassment by DeLuca: pointing to the bulge in his trousers and commenting to a student, "this is what you do to me"; telling a student, "you're a cock teaser when I thought you would be a cock pleaser"; asking a student if she ever "sucked on a man's dick"; suggesting that a student list her assets on an application form as "a nice ass, nice tits and a good lay"; constantly staring, smiling and winking at a student; commenting on how beautiful or pretty students were, or that they had a "nice ass" or "big chest" or "big boobs"; commenting that he intended to teach a student how to kiss or that he wanted to be the first male to kiss a student; indicating to a student that she would get high marks if she slept with him; encouraging a student to take his class, assuring her that she would do well and her marks would be high; asking a student if she was "horny"; noting that a student was wearing a bra and attempting to guess its size; and threatening to deny a student permission to go on a school field trip if she didn't go into a supply room, for an inappropriate purpose, with him.

Some might speculate that given his age and proximity to the culprit, perhaps Bad Doug was himself a victim of DeLuca. But surely if such had occurred, this would have been the transgression that set off alarm bells among the dozens of Catholic District School Board principals, secretaries, janitors, and passing light-bulb salesmen the many heterosexual abuses were reported to. If he'd been rutting and complimenting and squeezing boys, surely Fred Mills, the Catholic Board's Director of Education from 1968-1978, wouldn't have instructed his wife to "pray" for DeLuca because he had "a problem," while not instructing his spouse to pray for the dozens of girls getting their breasts squeezed and their bra sizes guessed at and rutting noises made against their pelvises.

I whispered a few words to Capp. We flew about enlisting neurodivergents to print DeLuca-relevant documents that would fuel Bad Doug B's righteous anger. Of course there should have been a hell of a lot more, but the *Sault Star* lacked the resources to digitize their two centuries of pre-digital content, including, as it were, *The Story of Baw-a-ting: Being the Annals of Sault Sainte Marie*, published by Sault Star Press, 1903. No, instead of digitizing all that, pretty much every red cent the place was bringing in went to pay Bob Stickman's $45,000-a-year salary. In fairness, a lot of the documents were available on microfiche, but that would have been asking a bit much of a neurodivergent given the antiquated nature of the technology, and also given that the archivist acted as a sort of gatekeeper to the microfiche machine and could be a real snot to anyone not well-versed in how to load and spin the defective old relic.

"Jesss-ihhhhh-caaaaaaaaaa," hell howled Doug.

I made up a lie on the spot, confident that Bad Doug B was too enraged and innervated and more a force of nature than a rationally-thinking wraith to clue into my ruse.

"Don't shoot the messenger here, Bad Doug," I remarked, "Fact is she's being tortured for eternity by DeLuca in his little after-world sex office. No one has been able to find the office, but if you listen closely, you can hear the rutting noises."

Of course the only rutting noises to be heard were the sounds of the actual rudders of the Army Corps of Engineers, but Bad Doug B was fairly suggestible in his condition. My hope was to marshal as much of Bad Doug B's rage as possible. For in the vengeance-oriented Wraith of Bad Doug Bindi, through some toxic offshoot of the malicious seed spread by DeLuca, we might wield some ugliness nearly commensurate to the evil of Dr. Sacks.

All the while, this same Dr. Sacks had been honing his influence on one Operator Derrickboat Derrick White of the Army Corps of Engineers. It's a little confusing that his given name is Derrick and his position is Operator Derrickboat. Such are the happy accidents enjoyed by the literary journalist.

For the layperson: Derrickboat Derrick operated a lattice boom/hydraulic crane. In the Corps hierarchy, Double D took his orders from the branch chief or his assigned master. Dr. Sacks wasn't even mentioned in the Corps chain of command.

And while this position was "covered by the civilian drug abuse testing program, and the incumbent [was] required to sign a DA Form 5019-R, Condition of Employment for certain civilian positions identified as critical under the Drug Abuse Testing program," Derrickboat Derrick was from the boring old upper peninsula of Michigan, and named Derrick after all, so what less could be expected? Of course he was addicted to opiates, and of course he was buying squeaky clean child urine to pass his tests, and of course he had no problem perjuring his way through a few

DA Form 5019-Rs, making him nice and susceptible to Sacksian nod-offs at the most crucial junctures of a crane man's day, for example, during the hydraulic craning of a 50-tonne piece of stone revenanting.

As Derrickboat Derrick's eyes fluttered and then closed, as his hand slipped forward on his crane joystick, this stone revenant's mass tumbled and counterproductively eroded a square kilometre of soil into the St. Mary's River, really weakening *corps d'esprit*.

It was on March 21, the first day of spring, that City Hall fell into the St. Mary's River, forcing Bob Stickman to write his first story on the situation, asking if maybe the town was experiencing some kind of mass delusion. I had laughed then, floating with Big Rog and Mellissa in the grease haze above a deep fryer at the Esquire Club.

"Whenever has this town not been suffering a mass delusion?" I asked.

A domino effect ensued. Into the river went the Korah Public Library, and let's hope that languorous archivist went with it. Into the River went the Station Mall with its laser tag arena and its action movies. Into the river went the Essar Centre, home to the Soo Greyhounds, the town's lone point of pride during these final years. Into the river went all the photos of Wayne Gretzy in his Hounds jersey: the Great One.

Essar Steel, once owned by Clergue, now operated by an offshore company that paid their municipal taxes with a whimsical bent, and were thought to be bankrupting the town while sending profits back to their native soil much as the town clerk had feared during the Depression: into the river, along with the 2,000 they employed!

Soo Foundry, also a Clergue brainchild. What do you think happened? Of watercourse into the river it went.

And surely it's not just structures falling into the river. Human beings are falling into the river, such is the speed of the erosion. These beings would be standing a solid ten feet from the river, then finding the ground beneath them increasingly mushy, then an unwelcome dampening of the loafers, then belt buckles, then shoulders, until a swimming motion became vital to sustained oxygen intake, and then it's off with the tide towards the state of Minnesota where based Bob Dylan was born.

Folks fled in terror. Second Line and Trunk Road were congested with traffic. A good deal of honking. Like honking has ever accomplished anything. Deb Martin was desperately trying to make a left turn against traffic out of the Walmart, leading to increased gridlock and increased screaming and then increased punching. All because of Deb valuing the greatest possible good over the practical, as though making a left turn out of that Walmart at any ever-lovin' time, let alone during a time of catastrophic erosion, was within the realm of possibility.

The addicted and *ergo* bicycle-proficient made it out better than anyone. Once they'd biked along 17N to Wawa they were safe; Dr. Sacks had no Wawaean beef. Then, however, the bicycling addicts found themselves situated in Wawa. What good was being in Wawa? Many texted Acne Allan asking if he could hit up Wawa anytime soon, preferably in the next quarter hour.

My dad packed the car and activated the seat rimjob mechanisms. My mother made a number of sandwiches and filled a cooler with juice boxes. David googled heroin tapering schedules. An anxious Maisie chewed Oxys provided a few days previous by Darby, who, in recent hours—and to the eventual profound sadness of both Andie and the Wraith of Mellissa Gladstone—actually had fallen into the river.

The wraiths of Big Rog, Mellissa, Capp, and myself took it all in, floating above the ever-encroaching coast line. It was like something out of a Michael Bay disaster movie. At least biblical doom was alive in Ba-wa-teeg.

"You know what I'm hoping . . . " said the Wraith of Big Rog.

"That your mom doesn't fall into the river?" asked the Wraith of Mellissa.

"Not exactly," responded the Wraith of Big Rog, "I am hoping that when this shithole falls into the drink, it will mess up that windbreak deal and by tomorrow we'll all be hanging out in sunny Florida like we were Cliff Claven."

"A dull and lugubrious climate for a baseborn pederast," remarked Capp. "Consider winter here—*when the leaf hath fallen and the sky grown grey and heavy, and the land wrapped in white enshrouding stillness*, consider those fine hours here before decamping for your suntan and your beach bingos."

"Those weren't bad hours," spoke Big Rog, sounding about as contemplative as Big Rog ever got.

I considered my own winters in Pawateeg, stepping out of the house and into the crunching snow en route to some warm Italian house, greeted by warm Italian mothers, offered cookies, Sambuca even, kissed even, all in the holy Sault Sainte Marie household afternoon. All before the Oxy came, all before the town fell into the gloom of Dr. Sacks.

Among the exodus south, some had cottages at Patton Lake they could retreat to. Some, God help them, were so hard up that they went to Sudbury, once described by CNN as a "wasteland" due to the town's industrially-wrought scourge of acid rain. Many, particularly those opiated parties on bicycles, would make it no farther than Garden River.

I'd like to apologize for not incorporating more of the First Nations' experience into this narrative. Certainly Sault Sainte Marie was founded on the arrival and the sustained efforts of Indigenous peoples, but given that I rely on Capp for the majority of my historical *bona fides*, and given that Capp has a problematic tendency of referring to these people as "savages" or "red men," and given the necessary zeitgeist of cultural sensitivity, I figured the less said of "savages" and "red men" the better. It's a tricky business, even for a posthumous author. Leave the good Ojibway of Garden River out of the narrative and you've whitewashed them out of Baw-a-ting's history when they named the place Baw-a-ting in the first place. Jerk move, truly. Depict them in the same honest light as all the molecule-dependent and daughter-diddling residents of Sault Sainte Marie and progressive publishers will recoil at the Brapster's manuscript submission in horror. Write in some wizened chief clicking his tongue at Saultite folly and that's the worst kind of cultural appropriation.

Capp wishes to interject to say that terms like "red man" and "savage" were merely the terms used to describe what he considered the savage and red men of his era. I rebutted that Capp had himself, on only the second page of his book, asserted, *Certain, however it is that the Indian, rude in habit, simple in life, and having little inventive genius, save in the matter of torturing his victims, is not connected with . . . the progress of a nation toward civilization,* and added that the *midnight surprise, the devilish war-yelps, the crushing of skulls, the tearing of scalps from struggling victims were the common features.*

Regardless of problems posed by Capp's internalized racism, the good Ojibway of Garden River were foisted into our narrative. As the bike peddlers grew winded, as minivan passengers' subconscious dread of the windbreak told them, "Drive no further," caravans of Sault Sainte Marie refugees stopped in the small reservation, home to 2,134 people, the birth soil of Stanley Cup champion Jordan Nolan as well as the painter David B. Williams.

As they'd often been at first contact, at least before all the smallpox blankets and squaw-rapings put a damper on things, the residents of Garden River were bemused hosts, gracious if a little puzzled. As an acquaintance of the authors, Thomas Pynchon, wrote in *Mason & Dixon:*

> All the people, even Nations far to the South and the West, dreamt you before ever we saw you,—we believ'd that you came from some other World, or the Sky. You had Powers and we respected them. Yet you never

dream'd of us, and when at last you saw us, wish'd only to destroy us. Then the killing started,—some of you, some of us,—but not nearly as many as we'd been expecting. You could not be the Giants of long ago, who would simply have wip'd us away, and for less. Instead, you sold us your Powers,—your Rifles,—as if encouraging us to shoot at you,— and so we did, tho' not hitting as many of you, as you were expecting. Now you begin to believe that we have come from elsewhere, possessing Powers you do not—Those of us who knew how, have fled into Refuge in your Dreams, at last. Tho' we now pursue real lives no different at their Hearts from yours, we are also your Dreams.

Or as Chief Waabojiig said when John Johnston was wooing his daughter Ozhaguscodaywayquay, "White Man, I have noticed your behaviour, it has been correct; but, White Man, your colour is deceitful. Of you, may I expect better things?"

They fed us venison, but also less stereotypical offerings such as macaroni and cheese. And sure, some were surly over having already been betrayed by the Lake Superior Treaty of 1850. And sure, some were drunk or opiated, as any percentage of any population must be. But on the whole there was a general spirit of merriment on the occasion. Maybe we Saultites might consider appropriating some of their strategies for dealing with tragedy. Got to laugh before you can cry, type thing.

None of this easy camaraderie sat well with Deb Martin when truths remained unreconciled. The consummate concerned party, Deb would wring her hands for your cause whether you wanted her to or not, *with the unreasonable spirit, born no doubt of eagerness for the triumph of the cause, but which has unfortunately characterized the religious enthusiasts of every age.*

Not an hour after arriving at the Community Centre, she'd commandeered a card table, cardboard, and a magic marker to set up the "Friends of Garden River Anti-Colonization League."

She was taking signatures. Signing meant you'd be anti-colonization. Not signing meant you'd be all in on colonization, in Deb's books, which only meant she had to educate you, so as to alleviate your ignorance. Most of the Sault refugees fell into this ignorant camp, too concerned about their lost homes and livelihoods or drowned and Minnesota-bound relatives to care about Deb's grandstanding. The Ojibway hosts didn't care for Deb Martin speaking out against colonialism on their behalf either. As Deb herself might have said of a rival, "She was taking up too much space in the conversation." Deb went largely ignored until she started handing out needles loaded with Xalisco boy heroin because she hadn't had time to order Anti-Colonization League-branded tote bags. These needles drew unruly crowds of Ojibway and Sault Du Gaston folx to her table until one of the Garden River elders politely asked Deb to leave, causing Deb Martin to accuse this elder of being herself an agent of colonialism, leading to Deb Martin being the only person arrested by the Garden River Tribal Council that day.

Since there's absolutely nothing along Highway 17N for ten hours until Thunder Bay, those fleeing in that direction found their earliest point of refuge at Searchmont Ski Hill and Resort. Searchmont sold a lot of Northern Superior draft beer on this day. Some even skied to pretend nothing was happening, erosion-wise. To some extent, Searchmont has always provided this illusion of escape for us. To be in a snowy chalet—you might have been in Maine; you might have been in some fine place.

Among the seasons pass holders there was a touchy and exclusionary vibe at first, like, "Hey, this is a ski hill not a homeless shelter," but as the people poured in and night fell, eventually Searchmont staff were forced to set up cots in the lodge, really marring the once-upscale exclusivity of the lodge.

Children were amassed. Some were kept occupied on the bunny hill. Those that could snowboard were told to do so. I was relieved to see Adelle arrive with her family. Within minutes she'd corralled those from her class to provide them with some sense of normalcy.

"So is the town completely in the river?" asked that

unwitting descendent of Ermatinger.

"Bob Stickman is reporting that everything up to Second Line is gone," said Adelle.

"If we can't go back to the Sault, will we live here at Searchmont forever?" asked a pie-eyed optimist.

"That probably wouldn't be sustainable," said Adelle.

"Will we be put in homeless shelters, because we're homeless now? I heard from my cousin who is a social worker but hates being a social worker that homeless shelters all smell like piss, I mean pee-pee," asked the cousin of a spiritually-compromised social worker.

"I don't think so. Maybe your parents can work in the part of town that's not in the river. Or they can get jobs somewhere else," said Adelle.

"Like Blind River?"

"Like Bruce Mines?"

"Like Elliot Lake?

"Like Espanola?"

"Stink town Espanola?"

"I don't want to live in stink town Espanola."

Because of its mining industry, Espanola smelled of sulphur, or, to the minds of children and low-brow non-fiction novelists—it smelled like farts. Espanola had always been the favoured whipping boy of we Saultites, because our town doesn't smell like farts and we had that to hold over somebody.

"I heard the Titans of Thor have taken over what's left of the Soo and they're ruling with an iron fist?" said a youth concerned with right-wing death squads.

"What's the Titans of Thor's deal anyway?" asked the mayor's nephew.

"Aren't they like racist foot soldiers?" asked a progressive child clued in to the racial supremacism always to be feared of the far right.

"No, they're just cleaning up the streets. Old fashioned values. Nothing racist about that," said a far-right apologist.

"I wanted to go home to get my iPad but then I saw on Facebook that the Titans of Thor are shooting first and asking questions later," said a child who valued his iPad just slightly less than his life.

"Yeah an iPad isn't worth that. It's just a piece of plastic, man. It's just like some circuits," said the ear expanders kid, elucidating how a commercial product is worth less than a human life.

"Except the iPad is like my window to the world, you know, get on WiFi, see what's happening everywhere else, watch my shows, not just be stuck at this ski hill."

"You can obviously just use someone's phone," said the class Stacey.

"Yeah, like once in a while but I can't like stream stuff or you know . . . " said the technology-addicted youth. "Like give me your phone right now and I'll catch up on all my YouTubers while you just sit there without a phone, how 'bout eh?"

"Are there any homeless shelters that give out iPads?" asked the homeless shelter-averse child whose social worker cousin had wearied of the piss smell and lost her idealism and realized the ideological framework provided in social work school didn't hold up against the ammonia-reek of urine that came to signify for her the dispiriting characteristics of the homeless.

Ear Expanders stood up on the couch for some reason, perchance to make the following seem more official: "Well, I'd just like to say, if we are all shipped off to various homeless shelters to get fleas and not have iPads, that it's been an exemplary thing to know each and every one of you. Ms. Salituri, you've been a noble and decent teacher, decent to the core. Stacey, I have always loved you, but I think you know that. We are good people. Saultites, ever. Now we must part ways to leave for the less eroded and swampy and non-Titans of Thor-dominated regions where life pulses on, where the scourge of sad . . . "

"Gay!" yelled Stacey.

"Yeah gay!" yelled someone else.

I found my family enjoying seat-warmer rimjobs along Highway 17S. Every fifteen minutes they had to pull over to allow for David's violent expectorations. Maisie, having less of a dependency but still struggling, kept asking my mom for a Tylenol Cold and Flu. My mom was keeping the remaining Tylenol Cold and Flus for David due to the nastiness of his cold.

In Bruce Mines they were greeted by my aunt and uncle. The fecal matter upon David's thighs and all up in his pants was hosed off in the back yard. Neighbours looked with reticence upon this shit-hosing.

My aunt made tea. A game of Balderdash was discussed but no one was up for the usual Balderdash baloney.

"How long until you can go back?" asked my uncle.

"Not sure what there's left to go back to," responded my dad.

"How's the lot?"

"In the St. Mary's River."

"What about your stock?"

"Insured."

"Erosion insurance?"

"Act of God, isn't it?"

Say what you will about Bruce Mines, with its population of 600 and its one restaurant, one hotel and one of everything, but the place still had Hydro, allowing Maisie to charge her phone and communicate with Jay and Andie.

> **MAISIE:** You guys just like I predicted I'm stuck in Bruce Mines. ☹

> **JAY:** That's actually kind of lucky because I'm in Garden River and Deb Martin's anti-colony league keeps doing drum circles.

> **MAISIE:** I'm not sure if drum circles are better or worse than Balderdash and my brother shitting his pants all the time. Andie is your dad still shitting his pants all the time?

> **ANDIE:** Oh wow is he ever. Worst part is because my dad was shitting his pants so much we never made it out, and then all the stragglers were rounded up by the Titans of Thor and now the Titans of Thor have kidnapped us all or are protecting us they say in some school but they're also reading their pamphlets about the white race and even accusing some Italians of not being part of the white race but if the Italians try to argue they just get tased or kicked in the teeth and stuff. Plus they started giving me all this heroin which was fun at first but now I'm super addicted FFS.

> **JAY:** Be safe hun!

> **ANDIE:** Some of the Titans of Thor keep giving me the eye it's really creepy.

This private message was then sent to Maisie outside of the group chat:

> **Jay:** Lol she actually thinks the Titans of Thor would want to wheel her when the Titans of Thor could probably wheel anyone they want right now.

I decided to check up on these Titans of Thor. After the Fentanyl Crackdown Unit had fled to Garden River and Searchmont to crack down on fentanyl in those locales, as unpoliced chaos descended on Baw-a-ting, the Titans found their role had expanded beyond street sweeping and needle collecting. To prevent the remaining dregs of the town from destroying each other, the Titans implemented some modest measures of control, measures the dregs would come to criticize as being more in line with the principles of human trafficking than good public policy.

Contraindicative of their aversion to needles and loose morals, the Titans oversaw a nascent prostitution/heroin economy, synthesizing the town's two great vices: opiates and DeLucaean living. Those who had heroin to spare, either because they didn't use heroin, or had so much heroin that to use it all themselves would spell their demise, were having so much DeLucaean sex that the sex itself became a bore, more of a chafing concern than an accomplishment.

"I need you to be more into it," said some Titan of Thor, quasi-consensually fornicating in an alley behind the

Nicolet Tavern with a youthful figure familiar to readers of this narrative.

This Titan of Thor wanted the nociceptively cold young woman to be warm for him in exchange for drugs. But it would never happen. Not with his Coors Light abdomen distended the way it was. Not with the hobo scent he was emitting. So the T.O.T. drank more of the Nicolet's dwindling beer supply, never wondering how it might be replaced with the just-in-time economy having been taken away, as so much had been slowly taken from the town over the years: half the movie theatre, the drive-in, the Korah Library's archives, even all the archivist's cardigans by then.

The Titans had a good thing going, with just enough heroin, just enough suckin' and fuckin', all just in time before the whole place was underwater, sucked into the fissure beneath the St. Mary's River, the void that had been sucking something from us all this time. Pawateeg, by the rapids, of the rapids—did it never occur to us that we owed a debt to these rapids, and that one day it would come due?

"This ain't worth a .5, " the Titan of Thor/human sex trafficker said to Andie's father outside the Nicolet.

And young Andie tried to feign warmth for the Titan of Thor, so that she and her father could get the heroin they needed. She was there abutting the Nicolet, affecting her child's caricature of sexual enthusiasm, because of a number of factors but primarily because of what the Sacklers had set forth.

And now, readers are encouraged to enjoy Bob Stickman's *Sault Star* reportage from the period:

City Council Cedes Control of SSM to Titans of Thor

In a controversial move, council voted 8-3 to disband council, revoke the mayor of his mayoral duties, and hand over city management to the Titans of Thor.

The Titans of Thor claim to be a civic-minded group.

Some believe the Titans of Thor are a white supremacist organization.

"Sex trafficking, drug running, thinly-veiled Nazi propaganda, is this the type of organization we want running our city?" said Deb Martin, president of the League of Concerned Citizens Opposed to the Titans of Thor, from her prison cell at the Garden River Tribunal Penitentiary and Rehabilitation Centre, where she is being held on charges related to her anti-colonialist position.

"Really, all we want to do is help," said Lars Goering, treasurer of the Titans of Thor. "It's a lot of fear-mongering. And with that soy-boy Prime Minister scared to send in the military again, who else is going to run what's left of this place? Don't listen to our words. Look at our actions. The streets are cleaner. Yes, we are running sex and drug rings, but do you want random prostitutes and drug dealers everywhere or do you want it run out of one central hub?"

The Titans of Thor Underage Prostitution and Heroin Centre is located at 443 Northern Avenue East, the former Sault College.

At this time, .1g bindles of heroin are going for a dozen canned food items. Adult prostitutes are available for .5g bindles of heroin. Prices for under-aged prostitutes remain negotiable, and are "based on appearance."

Goering urges remaining locals to make the best of what he calls "apocalyptic days in Sault Sainte Marie."

"Do some heroin. Fornicate with an under-aged girl without the state putting its long nose into your business if you get what I'm saying, and here I am referring to the International Jew."

⌘

Titans of Thor Rename Second Line to Hitler Boulevard

One of the city's main thoroughfares is getting a new moniker.

"We think Hitler did some things wrong, for sure, but then you look at all the good he did for Germany," said Ulrich Himmler.

The Canadian Jewish Council weighed in, calling the move "cause for massive alarm" on Twitter.

Deb Martin could not be reached for comment at her tribunal prison cell.

"Hey, if you don't like Adolph Hitler, don't drive on Adolph Hitler Boulevard. Take Mortimer Sackler Boulevard, formerly Third Line. It's not going to kill you," said Ulrich Himmler, minister of Communications for the Titans of Thor.

⌘

Town Motto Changed by Titans of Thor

The town's longstanding motto of "Sault Sainte Marie: Catch the Excitement" is getting a makeover.

According to Ulrich Himmler, communications czar for

the Titans of Thor, the new motto will be "Sault Sainte Marie: Now More Than Ever."

Deb Martin again could not be reached for comment.

"I think it's neat," said Andie Tomlinson, local teen prostitute. "Kind of gives us something to be positive about. Like the Soo is as good now as it used to be, but even more."

"There was some internal debate," chuckled Himmler. "Some argued that it's actually less now than ever because so much of the town has fallen in the river. But then the majority felt that it was more important to be positive than to get too bogged down by what the facts were on the ground."

At the Cambrian Mall, now an encampment for undesirables, I found the Wraith of Mortimer Sackler. Despite being a descendent of Polish Jewish immigrants, Morty was now manifesting as a swastika.

"Nice to see you've finally gone full heel," I remarked.

Sackler was too busy flowing hate into the hearts of the Titans of Thor running the Cambrian Mall/Centre for Undesirables to respond.

This was it, I thought. What didn't erode away would be razed by strategic air strike or something.

I'd long fantasized of the Sault's eradication from the earth. It had abandoned me, leaving me with no means of abandoning it. I'd long thought that only a thermonuclear device could get me free, never having fathomed the geologic might of Big Pharma wraiths.

The rupture occurred in the Christmas break of second year university. After the first year, some had returned from school having experimented with ecstasy. That summer ecstasy had offered a welcome alternative to the previous go-to of 24 cans of Molson Canadian per man. Preceding what's now known as Molly, when E was primarily speed and mystery ingredients, we had hugged and explained what we'd meant to each other, all fairly quotidian as the drug goes, except these were Triple A hockey-playing young men in Sault Sainte Marie, piercing the veil of Saultite bro insularity to reach the core of our affections for one another.

Everyone overdid it, *oh for sure eh*, and a year later these ecstasy parties had grown rote and dark. Most drank too much. Others crushed and snorted the pills for quicker onset. The pills burned badly upon insufflation. Once insufflated the insufflator would say, "Hospital? Hospital?" half-jokingly. The next person would snort their crudely-crushed pill pile to expose how much of a "pussy" the previous insufflator had been, until this person too would say, "Hospital? Hospital?" and the one sober guy was asking with increasing concern, "Do you guys seriously need to go to the hospital?" We never did. The fake drugs we were painfully snorting were our latest *tragic masks*, our latest incarnation of chair shots and comic writhing, Barthes' "ever-entertaining image of the sorehead, endlessly confabulating his displeasure."

We sat around and shared nothing. The drunks carried the day. The veil remained intact. We did not even listen to music. A *Fundamentals of Basketball* video was played. Young men boasted of their wheelings and of what recent violence they'd perpetrated. There is a male toxicity problem, make no mistake. Not just in Sault Sainte Marie but the world over. To avoid this burden of toxic males, I'd always endeavoured to be the most toxic male in any given situation.

As Dick Vitale threw a chest pass or something, Adelle Salituri had walked into the messy student home. I hadn't seen her in over a year. My face enlivened in a way that was inappropriately reverential. She gave me a wave to indicate, "You're already embarrassing me." She made idle chit-chat with the most toxic males until some vestigial chunk of the itself-toxic E manifested my sense of destiny. I asked Adelle to talk in the kitchen. I looked her in the eyes. Those green eyes. I squared the star incarnate up for a heart to heart. I hadn't yet learned that civilians, as a rule, lack the empathic forbearance to absorb/handle the artificially ecstatic persona.

"You're being weird," she said.

I was being weird. I suffered an awareness of this perceived weirdness. Yet I knew there was an *Onyx*ian monologue in me. It was my last chance. I cursed the set and setting. At Harmony Beach I'd have been sunglassed and less intense; Dick Vitale would have had nothing to say.

Adelle announced that she was leaving. With nothing to lose, I asked her for a ride. She lived only a few blocks from me. In the darkness of the car I could lower my head and make my case.

"I'm staying at Jodie's tonight," she said, which must have meant "no."

Adelle left. The twice-toxic males, unaware of her presence in my psyche, perceived my request for a ride home as a betrayal of our intended ecstasy bonding. The drinking grew heavier as it always does in Sault Sainte Marie. I stumbled out onto Trunk Road tundra and walked the fifty-five minutes to my parents' house. A few weeks after this my wisdom teeth were removed and I got my first Percocet prescription. It was but six months later I was hooked.

To revisit the site of your old hopes and realize they are no longer viable is an upsetting paradox. Those hopes never came to life, but they existed. This place, this home, had been lost in the process. I'd spoken a prayer then for my acquaintances, their torpor over-seasoned with irony, lost here in this wilderness abutting the Canadian Shield with nothing left to comfort them but Dick Vitale and pills initially presumed less toxic because they came from a pharmacy.

I had an out though. I didn't need to pray for myself. I could return to abundant Toronto. I could not look back, I told myself then, but then LOL all I've done since is look back in anger, and also in "haunting wild sorrow and regret," to quote another friend to the authors, Thomas Wolfe, because there is a magic door to happiness in Sault Sainte Marie that I found once but could never find again.

And now that Sackler had won the day I sought to say *adieu* to it all. Goodbye to Adelle Salituri and the thousand other Adelle Salituris adored and admired over the Sault's 160- to 2000- to 13.7 billion-year history, depending on one's historiographic bent. Think of all those Salituris. All those jaws and lips. Never again would this world know the Sault Sainte Marie angel face. No new children would know the pleasure of picking up groceries at Pino's on Christmas Eve, like a burst piñata of Yuletide glee, when the men referred to the parking lot as a *madhouse* and whistled apprehensively about so seasonally-late a trip to Pino's, suppressing their secret excitement over the challenge of parking in a madhouse for once. No more riding bikes and lighting fires in garbage cans, or stealing potted plants from elementary school sills. No more feeling the night in summer in Sault Sainte Marie, where the summer only lasts two and a half months, so should your Saliturian figure show up unexpected on some stoop while the cool fresh wind off Ke-che-gum-me mixed with the humidity, you might feel the mystic quality that first brought the Algonquin to Bow-a-Teeg in 15 B.C. or whenever. The games of capture the flag; the male friendships that grew estranged and all the lifetimes of unspeakable pain affected thereby; the girls, even the ones that weren't Adelle, did I mention them? Capp suggests that I have. The $2 cafeteria poutines. The drunken jaunts to the football game at sixteen when the air was a crisp -2 but a sweater would suffice and I'd hold a 4'10 cousin of Adelle in my arms and spend the next week imagining a new life with the cousin and my eventual betrayal of her with the foremost Salituri yet somehow they'd both end up loving me so I'd have to *Sophie's Choice* the diminutive cousin out of the equation. The voices; the shtick; the personal gimmicks—every town has these—none are particularly noteworthy or special, but then neither do any deserve extinction. It was all I'd known for the first nineteen years of my life. It had been all of those mystic things to me, so the Sault dying was akin to Bob Dylan dying. Some piece of magic that God had manifested in the world would cease to be, and so mark a point on the board for the Infernal Serpent. No more of all that. Thanks a pants load, Sackler, I thought.

I found the Wraith of Capp at Bellevue Park.

"Happy?" I admonished. "If you'd only cared less about our native soil this would never have happened. Sure, the slow decline would have continued, but city hall wouldn't be in the river and the neopagan far right wouldn't have quarantined undesirables. The lesson here, Capper, is since there's not a fucking thing that can be done, the worst thing you can do is to care about a place like Sault Sainte Marie. The worst goddamn thing."

"Sacrilege," said Capp in a weak voice, "All is not lost. For I have placed a message upon the wind."

"Oh shut up," I said. And after a moment, "We can

place messages upon the wind? Like a wraith telegram?"

"More akin to prayer," said Capp. "A sort of directed prayer."

"Oh, Rick Warren type stuff. Scarcely less of a con-man than Clergue."

I turned my back on Capp. I was manifesting my wisps in such a way as to figuratively pour one out for based Ba-wa-teeg when I heard that mighty train-whistle a blowin'.

The train was not a train per se. The train was the manifested hate wisps of Bad Doug Bindi.

"Huzzah!" cried the Wraith of Capp.

Two wispian figures sat in the engineer's compartment.

"Could it be?" asked Capp.

From Capp's electromagnetic crepitating and popping I knew that indeed it was, and that his message upon the wind had been heard.

"Sir Francis H. Clergue!"

"Who's the dandy in the flowing robes? Julius Caesar?" I asked.

"A Caesar of Ontario for certain. That is good Sir James Dunn, of whom, I must confess, I now regret speaking ill of earlier."

Quick *mea culpa* here: we've neglected to give Sir James Dunn the Clergue treatment up to this point in the narrative largely because Capp has such a boner for Clergue. Plus, just as I could not have predicted Bad Doug Bindi's untimely death, how was I, simply a reporter on the ground, to have foreseen Sir James Dunn's WWE-inspired run-in? Allow us to pause during so climactic a moment for a brief biographical sketch.

From *Courage,* a somewhat puffy biography written by Dunn's whimsically-named pal Lord Beaverbrook:

> By the development of ore bodies he fired all Canada with enthusiasm for exploration and research, sparking many projects that have increased and multiplied the mineral wealth of the country . . . His life story is a resounding example of what can be accomplished by men of mature years, for he showed that old age need impose no barrier to achievement, no limit to vision . . . Twice he was on the brink of ruin. He saved himself by his own efforts and his own strength of character . . . Twice he was in danger of death, when he sustained a coronary thrombosis, followed by a major operation in his 70th year.

More relevant to Baw-a-ting, from Wikipedia, and with apologies to those who hold this account to a higher standard of scholarship such that a Wikipedia quote is perceived as unbecoming and sullying, yet still it's pretty concise so deal with it:

> At the age of 61, Dunn engineered a takeover so that he became the sole controlling shareholder thereby allowing him to take the tough but necessary reorganization measures to restore profitability to [Algoma Steel]. To accomplish this, he raised capital by negotiating bank loans, selling his beloved art collection and taking stock instead of income. As Algoma Steel's president and Chairman of its board of directors, he successfully turned it into one of the largest steel mills of the day and for more than twenty years guided the fortunes of the company he would eventually make into one of the most profitable producers in Canada.

From Beaverbrook, *op cit,* as they say:

A dreamer of dreams.

Again from the Beav-man:

> One day, in a fairground booth, he won a boxing prize
> of ten dollars. This apparently chance happening changed
> the entire course of his life. For had James Dunn not been
> small and slight, he might not have been so eager to prove
> his worth against bigger men in the boxing ring. And had
> he not done so, then he would never have won this prize
> which his talent and energy multiplied a millionfold.

Anyway . . .

The train pulled into a figurative wraith station of
Dunn's making. It must have been Dunn rather than
Clergue who broke the wild buck of Bad Doug Bindi's
anger. Clergue appeared timorous, nothing more than a
self-conscious flim-flam man whose half-assed dreams for
Algoma had partially led to the ethnostate/fentanylic
hellhole the place had become.

And yet still the Wraith of Capp rushed to embrace
Clergue in a way that I considered unmanly of Capp, and
which only seemed to embarrass Clergue further.

Other members of the Baw-a-ting dream team emerged
from their train cabins.

"Ermatinger!" cried Capp, "So nice to make your
acquaintance. John Johnston, hello! Captain Roberts,
Alexander Henry, David Pim, Gitcheojeedebun, Père
Jacques Marquette, Parson MacMurray, Marie Du Sauveur,
Chief Waabojiig!"

Not thrilled with the Eurocentric depictions of his
peoples in *The Story of Baw-a-ting*, Chief Waabojiig
pretended to scalp the Wraith of Edward Henry Capp. That
broke the tension and we all had a good laugh about it.

The Wraith of Dunn rose above us all, *i.e.* the time for niceties was through. All very intimidating, as he was after all wearing the Caesar-style robe. This, Capp has informed me, was based on a portrait of Dunn that had been painted by Salvador Dalí. I'd known the public high school was named after Dunn. Had not known he'd warranted Dalí portraits. Shame on me for not boning up on the history of Pawateeg, I suppose.

"Point me to the devil!" spoke the Wraith of Sir James Dunn, apparently not one for excessive verbiage.

We all hopped aboard the Bad Doug Bindi express, destination: the Cambrian Mall/undesirables camp. The DeLucaean hatred pulsed and pushed us forward. This was the hatred that I could not tame. In this regard, I was like Clergue. I'd seen the raw potential, but had been unable to master the natural resources. We'd needed Sir James Dunn in the 1960s, and now we needed his *Courage* once more. Moreover, in a Vince Russo-tier *swerve*, we'd needed the city's top heel, Bad Doug Bindi, to make an improbable babyface turn.

As the train crashed figuratively through the walls of the Cambrian Mall, Sackler puffed up his swastika presence in response. He did tip a swastika stick in the direction of Dunn however, one billionaire to another, as Dunn's net worth would have easily exceeded the billion mark in today's currency.

To commence the battle, it was suggested that Chief Waabojiig, "known for his eloquence and poetry as well as his warlike daring" (Penny Petrone, *First People First Voices*), would be allowed to essay the war song that his warriors had chanted on the eve of many a bloody battle. The Wraith of Capp rolled his eyes; the Wraith of Dunn issued a paternal little nod of consent, and so in the noble spirit of the most heartfelt land rights acknowledgement, old Waabojiig essayed:

> Where are my foe? say, warriors? No forest is so black,
> That it can hide from my quick eye, the vestige of their track;
> There is no lake so boundless, no path where man may go,
> Can shield them from my sharp pursuit, or save them
>   from my blow.
> The winds that whisper in the trees, the clouds that spot
>   the sky,
> Impart a soft intelligence, to show one where they lie,
> The very birds that sail the air, and scream as on they go,
> Give me a clue my course to tread, and lead me to the foe.
>
> The sun at dawn, lifts up its head, to guide me on my way,
> The moon at night looks softly down, and cheers me with
>   her ray,
> The war-crowned stars, those beaming lights, my spirit
>   casts at night
> Direct me as I tread the maze, and lead me to the fight.
> In sacred dreams within my lodge, while resting on the land,
> Bright omens of success arise, and nerve my warlike hand.
> Where'er I turn, where'er I go, there is a whispering sound,
> That tells me I shall crush the foe, and drive him from
>   my ground.
>
> The beaming west invites me on, with smiles of vermil hue,
> And clouds of promise fill the sky, and deck its heavenly
>   blue,
> There is no breeze, there is no sign, in ocean, earth or sky,
> That does not swell my breast with hope, or animate my
>   eye.
> If to the stormy beach I go, where heavy tempests play,
> They tell me but, how warriors brave, should conquer in
>   the fray.

All nature fills my heart with fires, that prompt me on to go,
To rush with rage, and lifted spear, upon my country's foe.

Capp but not I would like to apologize for the length of the proceeding war song.

The battle was afoot! The train-Wraith of Bad Doug Bindi pounded into the Wraith of Sackler, reversed and pounded thrice more. Though shaken, the Sackler swastika only chuckled.

Then the common wraith-men emerged from the train's rear with wheelbarrows of hermatite ore and also another low-grade ore called siderite. These were the materials by which Dunn had reversed Algoma's fortunes in the 1960s. Mere siderite should have been useless against the Wraith of evil Dr. Sacks, especially as these elements were just imagined wraith wisp manifestations. They worked, we believe, due to what they talk about at Our Lady of Good Counsel, and that thing is called "the mystery of faith."

This faith was known to the region as far back as 1669, when *overcome with weariness, vexation and disappointment, the [Jesuit] Fathers, soon after their arrival, faltered in their work, but night brought to one of the little community a vision of the Blessed Virgin who gave assurance of protection and bade all take heart. After such an event it was only right that something should be done by way of commemoration, and so the name was changed from Sault du Gaston to that of Sault Sainte Marie.*

The wraith-men mostly believed in a Judeo-Christian God or else more of a Ke-che-mun-e-do-type deity; moreover, they believed in Dunn and they believed in the siderite and they believed in the hermatite more than they believed in the inevitable doom of Sault Sainte Marie. And to this end the Wraith of Sackler began to weaken and dissipate.

"Fuck you, Sackler!" I shouted.

"To the pit with you, old Nut Sack!" idiomatically winked the Wraith of Capp.

"I've wasted enough time in this dump," said Sackler. "Damage has been done. My name has been cleared. I have affairs in New York City."

"I'd wager," snickered Clergue, the consummate kick-a-guy-when-he's-down type.

As the Wraith of Sackler decamped, a change came over the faces of the Titans of Thor who'd been administering the low-grade torture upon those undesirables held in the Cambrian Mall detention centre. "What exactly are we doing?" conveyed the general facial expression. Some administrative Titans of Thor had a little *tête-à-tête*. They walkied some questions up the chain of command. Meetings were called for. The administrative Titans, after a second *tête-à-tête*, decided not to even wait for the meeting before releasing all the undesirables and issuing each with a handshake and frank apology.

Capp led the work wraiths in a round of huzzahs. The Wraith of Dunn dusted his hands rather pompously, but then he'd earned it, had he not? And the refrain of Kurt Vonnegut's *Timequake* came to mind: "You were sick, but now you're well again, and there's work to do."

I thought we should celebrate. As it turned out, it was Good Friday, and Capp and Clergue and Dunn were all pretty strict in their observances and only wanted to spend the day on which their Lord and Saviour Jesus Christ had risen from the grave by reflecting somberly upon their Lord and Saviour Jesus Christ's sacrifice.

On Holy Saturday the SSM dream team infiltrated psyches at Searchmont and at Garden River. We inspired methadone and buprenorphine programs among the molecule-dependent. We planted the seeds of civic reclamation projects among the more industrious.

By special request, we drove the train of Bindian wraith hate through David and through Maisie until they got the message Nancy Reagan was so ridiculed for, the one that maybe wasn't such a bad message after all: "Just Say No." But since just saying no wasn't enough in the face of heinous molecule dependence, we also drove home a pretty strict buprenorphine message for David but not for Maisie as Maisie didn't have all that serious of a habit.

"Do you think they can do it? These backwoodsmen? Can they rebuild it?" asked Clergue.

"Quit calling them backwoodsmen, you ghastly fop," bellowed Dunn, "To your question, the answer is yes. Should there be hermatite, should there be ore, it can be done."

"Besides," I said, "With the windbreak situation, they won't have much of a choice, will they?"

Dunn's wisp face took on a gravity.

"No man should be forced to stay in northern Ontario, not by economic hardship, nor by occult wind."

Thus the Bindian hate machine was driven to the outer boundaries of Bow-a-teeg, where, at Dunn's command, the men heaped hermatite and siderite on the boundary lines.

"Quite the visto," remarked the Wraith of Old Waabojiig, gazing back towards Baw-a-ting.

"I'd live and sup here, perchance," said the Wraith of Ermatinger, "Hard to know for certain, but surely I would ponder on it."

Big Rog made the scene and pretended to kick some dirt around.

"Listen, really grateful for all you've done, Mr. James," said Rog, "Just to clarify, we're free to go, right?"

"You don't have to ask my permission," said the Wraith of Sir James Dunn.

"Do I have to ask Cler-gay's permission?" asked Rog.

"Clergue is a failure and a charlatan," remarked Dunn.

Clergue didn't even argue.

The hermatite and the siderite and the faith they inspired was working. I took a wraith step outside of the boundary line.

The windbreak was depleted. The windbreak was destroyed. I looked to Capp. I half-expected a grimace of disappointment, as a career civil servant grimaces when he's finally free from civil servitude, but free to what? This grimace I did not find. All that remained of the Wraith of Capp were those little particles of dust that the Road Runner so often left in his wake.

I followed across the International Bridge, through Christmas, Cadillac, and Manistique, until we reached the closest population hub from Pawateeg: Detroit, Michigan. (Although, really, Toronto is equidistant, so I guess in Capp's living days Detroit would have been the superior hub.)

Arriving on Easter Sunday, we found the streets somewhat desolate. Starved for culture as he was, Capp consulted tourist brochures and we were soon ensconced in the Detroit Institute of Arts. It was free to residents of Wayne County and relatively full. A trio of obese hipsters played electronica with saws and some gimmick wherein wires extruded "randomly" from an antique synthesizer. It must have been the hipster epicentre of the world in that moment. I realized then that Capp had never truly experienced the twenty-first century hipster, amorphous a term as it's become, as this means of living had never quite taken hold in Sault Sainte Marie, with the possible and lone exception of the ear-expanded youth, and even he was just grasping in the dark.

Capp breathed it all in. He flitted about the hipsters,

through the beards and the belly-shirts. He infiltrated and investigated the synthesizer. He gazed into the eyes of a child affected by saw-synth. The child wore a look of wonder that no flash mob had ever generated, not once.

And then to the paintings. Van Gogh and Cezanne and all the lesser known masters. Great religious vistos half the size of the Korah Library. Christ bleeding to death. Little baby Christs bathed in light halos. Because of his invisibility, no security guard could stop Capp from getting right in amongst the paint. And this he did. And this I did. It was the time to make the most of our afterlives. We were free from Baw-a-ting. We rubbed our wraith faces on *Sylvette* by Picasso. We wraith-gazed upon *The Window* by Matisse.

"See, he broke it down! This Picasso, he broke it all down," cried the Wraith of Capp.

We took a tour of Detroit's dilapidation, hosted by a man who kept warning his patrons of potential car-jacking. We went to the Ghost Bar on the third floor of the Whitney Mansion, branded as being haunted, where we encountered not a single Motor City wraith.

We attended a Detroit Tigers baseball game. There was Mikie Mahtook walking around in circles after fouling off a tough pitch. They played *Take Me Out to the Ball Game* and then they played a song by Miley Cyrus, which must have been some new branding strategy inflicted on the populace by the dying music medium. Francisco Cervelli hit a routine grounder to short and was thrown out by a country mile. It would have seemed pretty boring except Capp and I knew that the Tigers and the Bucs would each do this 160 more times. All these grounders and loopers and murderous come-backers to the mound would consume half of a calendar year. There'd be developments. Francisco Cervelli would die of a brain embolism behind the plate and the Pirates would dedicate their season to the horror of that. Miguel Cabrera would get back on the booze and sully the Tigers' already-dubious pursuit of the second wildcard. "Filmmaker, actor, and recording artist" Vincent Gallo would inexplicably throw out the first pitch of a May 17 Wednesday afternoon game.

"Shall we return to Baw-a-ting?" I asked.

"I'm never setting hair nor hide in that shithole again," remarked the Wraith of Edward Henry Capp.

"Oh come on."

"I'm just roasting you," said Capp.

My family was among the first civilian parties returning to town. My mother was, as ever, leery. My father led the charge. Also, here was a chance to assert the patriarchal influence that the twenty-first century so seldom demanded of its 54-year-old men, to make a stand.

Sure, some were never to return, what with so many properties having fallen into the river, but more than half the population did come back. They brought with them the good old-fashioned work ethic that had built the machine shop and the mill and the steel plant in the first place.

And like the Algonquin, *in the Spring, those who survived the rigour of Peboon (winter), returned to Baw-a-ting by hundreds and having seen their krall-shaped wigwams pitched by their squaws, joined in the orgies and dances decked out in their most gaudy garb. Feasts and pow-wows lasted many days.*

Pino supplied these feasts, gratis. And with the blooming of spring, the fragrance of Pino's garlic sausages perfumed the unsunken suburbs. There came the sense of renewal that always came so late to Sault Sainte Marie, for our Aprils were no better than our Februaries, and only by May 2-4 might we consider wearing shorts.

In place of pow-wows, we held five flash mobs a week. Attendance was poor.

Non-repentant Titans of Thor were imprisoned and ridiculed. An anti-Titans of Thor Task Force was formed.

My brother, through the last of his withdrawals, had been scared straight. I noticed he was playing *Call of Duty: Black Ops 4* with altogether less enthusiasm. He'd played *COD4* with the highest achievable level of joy and now he'd accept less forever. He'd take up running, or vegan dining, and tell himself those choices made him feel as good as a molecule. He'd be lying to himself for the rest of his life.

Andie tried to forgive her father for human trafficking her to the Titans in exchange for heroin, but would struggle with that for some time. ☹

The Cambrian Mall was refurbished. I guess nobody wanted to go to the same Coles that had been the previous headquarters of the Undesirables Detainment Unit, so we ended up getting a slightly nicer Coles. The food court expanded to include both a Quiznos and a Pita Pit, which seemed like a redundancy of sandwich-based eateries. The entire 80,000-square-foot Canadian Tire was repurposed into a *Labour Day Store!*, which, sadly hindered by construction snafus, opened several weeks after Labour Day.

Margaret's husband suffered a heart attack, and though he did not die, the lineup of well-heeled 60yo+ suitors suddenly hanging around both the veterinary office and Margaret's home was numbered in the dozens. Suitors also flitted about the dying husband's hospital bed under the auspices of support, but their motivations were clear to my mom and the nurses and the doctors, which doctors were themselves giving Margaret the eye more often than not.

Speaking of dating, in a happy development, after breaking up with Mellissa, Big Rog started dating older women. Older wraith women that is. "I swear, these women, just as they're starting to lose it, they become youthful again. I'd say it has something to do with hormones, but do we even have hormones when we're dead?" he said to me over deep fryer fumes one evening. Big Rog is dating the Wraith of Deb Martin, who was killed by highwaymen following her release from the Garden River Tribunal Council, just before the town started getting its act together, meaning there were still bands of murderous highwaymen to contend with.

The Wraith of Rex also found contentment in the afterlife, viciously haunting the homes of various *Intervention* producers and A&E executives, rattling chandeliers, slamming doors, spooking beloved and wraith-sensitive pets and so forth, saying things like, "Know how you say at the start, 'These people know they are in a documentary about addiction but they do not know they will soon face an Intervention.' I mean come on, there was nineteen seasons, probably one of the sound guys has an A&E hoodie on, or else one of the PAs worked on *Little People, Big World* and he's wearing a Matt Roloff-branded golf shirt. And you know how the show is always shaming like the old grandma or the mother or the sister for being an enabler, for letting the addict live in their home and borrow $140 every morning. Well, isn't the show itself the greatest enabler of them all, because finally someone is forced to listen to the addict's molestation woes or whatever and it's like, 'Hey, I'm going to skin-pop this .2 of heroin and talk about my molestation and this gaffer is forced to sit here and listen, unlike all my non-enabling relatives who doubt I was even molested in the first place since my stepmother is a generally decent woman and women don't statistically commit a whole ton of molestations and I am a gross junkie covered in scabs.'"

While in rehab, Acne Allan figured he might as well suffer through a couple months of Accutane, worsening his acne nearly to Charles Bukowski-levels, leading to serious scarring, leading to a life of horrific relapses and a steady march towards the grave for Acne Allan.

The Wraith of Mellissa Gladstone was rebuked by the Wraith of Darby, made available to her in wraith form after he drowned in the river. These days she can be found haunting the Ardene store in the Station Mall.

My father watched hundreds of baseball games without a great deal of discernible satisfaction.

Bob Stickman was nominated for a Pulitzer Prize for his coverage of the erosion/opiate/Titans of Thor fiasco. Just kidding. He was also killed by highwaymen. ☺

A thirst for dark ecstasy brought tourists to bear witness to what tangible evils had been haphazardly documented by the archivist.

Three of the original members of Styx played the Essar Centre.

Rotary Days came in June.

Bon Soo came in February.

And life would continue on in Pawateeg.

I would like to thank Edward Henry Capp in the editorial interning, dream-downloading, and spiritual oversight of this work, and to this end, I would also like to give him the last word:

> Men who lived before the town took so lately its sudden leap into prominence sigh for the "good old times" that preceded these present, while those who were among the settlers of forty years since, think with regret of the happy days of the "then," but old folks, whose age is measured at the four scores and over, sit by the fire of a Winter night with their progressive grandchildren about their knees, and as they recall from the past sweet memories of their childhood and youth in the (to us) misty years of the nineteenth century in Sault Sainte Marie, even those whose heads are bowed with the snows of many winters, think and speak longingly and lovingly of those times and feel that such a measure of happiness and content-ment as they knew then will not again be theirs until the final journey has been taken, the great divide been crossed, and they, at least, have entered the Blessed Ishpem-ing [Ojibwe for heaven].
>
> Even to the settlers of 1843-56 the Sault seemed as

though it were always to be a mere child among its sister towns, but behold, a greater town than many another unfolds more fully each days its glory to the view. May those who come after us to carry on the work which we now indulge in find our dreams quite fulfilled, and Baw-a-ting, midway between the oceans, the centre of the great lakes, an industrial centre and a loyal metropolis in a mighty and prosperous land. Adieu!

Forgive me Edward Henry Capp, for I have more to say. And forgive me reader, for I have misled you. Given my tendencies towards the shoddy and the negligent, I've probably misled you in a number of ways, but most significantly I lied about the consummation. I lied because talking about the consummation, fourteen years prior to the composition of this work, had spoiled my chance at lifelong happiness.

The consummation occurred after a visit Adele had made to Montreal, a French Immersion thing. There she got a glimpse of a dominance hierarchy dominated not by Triple A hockey players but gourmands and peerless wits and so forth. I'm sure some clichés came into effect. We were sixteen, that fine age.

Upon her return to the Sault she telephoned me. She rarely telephoned me. It was I who telephoned her. Now there was a new tone in her voice, as though we might be equals. She wanted to watch a movie. Even then, an idiot, wholly virginal, I knew what 16yos did when they watched movies. She sat close. I could feel her hip flesh against my hip bone. She smelled of something sugary that I can't name but would smell in Mac's Mart lines for the remainder of my sad life. She described her trip and its gourmands and its world-class wits. The telephone rang. I picked it up without holding it to my ear and clicked the receiver, terminating the call. Who was it? Who could ever care? She kissed me then, suggesting how it might be between us. I said we were like Cory and Topanga, which was topical at the time, but also kind of self-aware, like, "Yeah, I guess Pierre & Co. probably had better lines." Anyway, it was happening.

She suggested going upstairs to my bedroom. We traversed the kitchen. We traversed past any number of infant siblings. I opened my bedroom door. The year previous, in anticipation of so unlikely a triumph, I had stored away all of my action figures. Surely these would have queered the deal. Another figure waited to queer it, the deal; and this was my father. Because we'd been dominating the downstairs area with our anxiety-provoking teenage sexuality, he was watching the Blue Jays game in my room while my mother watched *Better Times Rerun* in her own. My father wore a look of surprise when I opened the door. Adelle wore a look of surprise and shame.

"What's the score?" I asked, and then I shut the door before he could answer.

"I should go," said Adelle, "This is weird."

"I know a good place."

We traversed the kitchen once more. We descended the stairs. Under these stairs my friend Ken Good and I had carved out a 2' x 2' hole so that the space beneath the stairs could be occupied as a fort. We'd carpeted the fort. We'd wallpapered it with pictures from *Thrasher Magazine*. This was when *Thrasher* was read by real or at least aspirant skateboarders and not just a tired-out "iconic" T-shirt worn on alternate Wednesdays by the ear expanders kid.

"I'm not going in there," she said.

"It's nice," I said, "There's carpet. Ken and I built it."

She may have been concerned that she would not fit through. As described in the "bones"/"yokozuna" exchange, she was full-figured then, and at sixteen, a woman. Whereas I, at sixteen, weighed about 135 and had the facio-skeletal characteristics of a boy.

I crawled in. For a terrifying moment she hesitated, but there was nothing left for her to do but follow. I said some lines that might not have been Sturges-tier, but at least "cute" by Sault Sainte Marie standards. We resumed our passions. Years of anticipation and night hopes seemed to manifest in the chemical composition of lip gloss.

I touched the body parts I'd long longed to contact. Talk of tumescence might spoil the emotional impact of this passage, but thus it was achieved. The *wheeling*, a first for me, proved daunting, but insertion, not a first for her, was something she knew had to be worked at. I was in. The only place I'd ever wanted to be. There was just enough space that I could maneuver without bonking my head on any stairs. There was just enough light to see the serenity upon her face.

"I love you," she said.

"I've loved you since that night we limbo'd," I said.

"I love you," she said a bunch of times more.

After having been one, we became two again. Some rudimentary wiping. We decamped. She smiled at the 2' x 2' point of egress, the handiwork of Ken Good and myself.

"It's a magic door," she said.

"Will you be my girlfriend?" I asked her.

"I will," she said.

The next day was the first day of grade eleven, and maybe I told a few too many people about it, and maybe as

I tried to hold her hand in the cafeteria she was given pause, requesting a small amount of space, until the social hierarchy learned of this imbalance and assigned some lumbering and concussion-prone Double-A goon to steal her away. And who were we, just kids, to go up against all of that? There was no breakup, no saying goodbye, and after a dignified period of time lasting not longer than a semester, I resumed my supplicant position as lovable clown and water-logged paperback missing its front fifteen pages. The night of the magic door was only brought up when I was drunk at parties, where she would be forced to say, "Tom, you're embarrassing me."

Here lies the meagre wound at the heart of all my belly-aching and Sault Sainte Marie denigrating: a youthful love barely consummated. To have loved Adelle over a lifetime would have devolved into something mundane as mere interpersonal comfort. To never have had her, the longing might have faded. It was to have known her so briefly, at the perfect apex of teenage romanticism, and worse, to know that she too had known, and that she'd either forgotten, or simply preferred not to make the sacrifices required to tolerate a man of my "unique gifts and challenges" over a prolonged period—all this caused my love to fester and grow malignant. And this is what I feel for the birth soil of Sir Edward Henry Capp and myself, little place goes by the name of Pawateeg—I feel a malignant love that can never be excised.

If one last excess may be permitted, coincidentally, *The Story of Baw-a-ting* features this folk song from *La Belle France* that was heard in the lowly log home of early Sault Sainte Marie:

1

To thee, my sweet Adelle,
I've come to say Adieu
A year must drag its weary length
'Ere I may meet with you.
Pray for me, then my love, Adelle
And think of me as true

2

Ah! when you've paddled far
And touched the island shore,
Your heart some island belle will seize
You'll think of me no more
No longer will my voyageur
His poor Adelle adore.

3

Fie on thee now, Adelle,
Have I not promised thee?
Take thou my constant love
And give thy heart to me,
And my voyage ends, Adelle
We'll gladly married be.

Maybe it's not perfect. Maybe it doesn't suit my narrative. We wouldn't meet again in a year. We wouldn't *gladly married be*. Still, there seems to be some significance in the log home-dwellers singing sad songs of their own Adelle, and so I dream-downloaded it into the neurodivergent girl and had her hand it in as part of a history project.

Adelle saw it, smirked at the same name, and moved on with her marking. She had no reason to associate it with me. She had the very essence of the future around her: children. That was the secret of living in Sault Sainte Marie.

It didn't even matter if it was an illusory future, if the children were all bound to fall into a river or consume $C_{17}H_{19}NO_3$ molecules. That's where confirmed bachelors like Clergue and Capp and myself were at a loss. No children to watch grow. I might view a future vicariously through nieces and nephews, but truly what future is that? What would remain? Our haunting was to view the past eternal. That's why Capp had gotten so good at it; that's why he was so much more committed to archival works than the loathsome Korah Library Archivist, damn him.

The thought of all that Clergue-obsessing wearied me. I had to forget about the Nicolet Tavern being her favourite tavern and the sounds of skateboards on fresh-poured driveways; the Sears frottage irking the heteronormative functionary; the NVT game, which I really was so good at; the perfect bodies that Radiohead sang of, and how I could relate to Thom Yorke, insofar as me wanting them too; the negatively-charged ions at Hiawatha; the sex-charged dance ions; the drive-in movie theatre, the bras unclasped and the warm beers we drank there; the night, oh the mildness of the summer night; water-skiing assholes, even; more beers on the back deck; ordering pizza in advance of *Monday Night Raw*; all-night Bond-a-thons; the scuttlebutt around the first arrest of Big Rog; the way St. Thomas Elementary smelled on the first day of school; the coming of the fair each spring; the fistfights by the train tracks; the swinging dicks in the Greyhounds locker room that I once witnessed as a child; sprinklers in summertime and the refraction of sunlight therein. I was already dead, no sense regurgitating it again and again throughout a bloated afterlife of ceaseless recall. It was time to put Baw-a-ting or whatever you want to call it behind me, to hang up my sorehead's singlet, for as Barthes knew, "In wrestling, as on the stage in antiquity, one is not ashamed of one's suffering, one knows how to cry, one has a taste for tears."

And so *Adieu,* Sault Sainte Marie, Sault du Gaston, Pawateeg, Baw-a-ting, Bawitigong, you old Steel Town Down, you old heartbreaker. And to finally, yes, finally bring it all back home, and to give the last or at least penultimate word to our Ojibwe pals, *Gaa wiin daa-aangoshkigaazo ahaw enaabiyaan gaa-inaabid,* which means, "You cannot destroy one who has dreamed a dream like mine," so what's a little colonialism? What's twenty-one years of wickedness? What's a greed-driven epidemic of death and sorrow when you've dreamed a dream like ours?

ABOUT THE AUTHOR

MICHAEL SAUVE has written for *The National Post*, *Variety*, and *McSweeney's*. His five novels from Montag Press include *I Ain't Got No Home In This World Anymore* and *The Apocalypse of Lloyd*.